I0522363

We Can Fix America

By

Robert M. Crowder

Copyright 2011 by Robert M. Crowder
Second Edition

All rights reserved. No part of this book shall be reproduced, stored in a retrieval system, or transmitted by any means without written permission from the author.

International Standard Book Number: 978-0-578-09165-5

Dedication

This book is dedicated to my wife, Kellie, and my children, Brooke and Sterling. They have listened to me ramble about politics for the last four years. While at times they were bored of my "lectures," they have patiently listened, as I describe my opinion on how to fix America. I love each of you, and this book is dedicated to you.

Preface

Since the end of 2006, the American economy has been on a downward spiral. Substantial wealth has evaporated, and the American dream of home ownership has just about been blown away like dust. While it is easy to blame the current president or Congress, the reasons for the implosion are much harder to assess. It requires that we look in the past and some cases look at ourselves to find the answers. What is truly remarkable is that the clues were there to identify the collapse, but those in power failed to communicate what they knew was coming.

Over the last four years, I have taken more interest in our political system. As I have reviewed the many challenges facing our country, I have been amazed at the partisanship of our elected leaders. I have been equally baffled by their unwillingness to clearly communicate the pending doom that awaits America. America's financial system is on life-support, and politicians are more concerned about their own self-preservation. Without substantial changes in our political system, I am worried about the future of this country.

The following book is the first part of a series that I plan to write. This book plants the foundation on which the others will be built. While the characters and overall storyline are fiction, the underlying issues and discussions are very much true. I sincerely hope that you will enjoy this book, but I would much rather you gain an understanding of the challenges facing our nation today and the best solutions to fixing these problems.

Chapter 1

John looked at the lights from the train coming into the station. It was a sight that he had seen many times. He watched as the lights came closer and closer. He felt the biting wind that the train whipped up on cold fall mornings. He sipped his coffee and firmly clutched his laptop bag. The train doors opened, and John and his fellow platform friends hurried onto the car.

John was fifty-five year old living in Norwalk, Connecticut, with his wife, Jenny. For the last thirty years, he had taken the train into Manhattan to go to work at Smith Goldman, one of the largest investment banking firms in the world. At his usual departure time of five forty-five a.m., John knew today was a truly different: it was going to be his last day.

John had graduated from the College of William and Mary in Williamsburg, Virginia, in 1978 with a bachelor's in finance and from Wharton School of Business in 1981 with an MBA. He started at Smith Goldman on the trading floor as an analyst shortly after graduating from Wharton. In 1988, he moved into the investment banking side of the business, becoming one of the youngest vice-presidents ever. He became president of the US operations in 1996 and became the firm's forty-second chairman in 2002. John had performed extremely well as chairman, and the company had become the tenth largest investment banking firm in the world with worldwide deals totaling $150 billion in 2010. John had also amassed a large personal fortune estimated to be around $900 million.

John was known for his work ethic. He arrived at the office around six thirty every morning, worked through lunch most days, and left the office around six thirty each night. Typically, he answered e-mails or phone calls until around ten p.m. and during the weekends. There were legendary stories that, around deal closings, John could be found in the office as many as five days in a row without going home. Jenny would courier over a change of clothes.

John and his wife had purchased a winter chalet in Aspen, Colorado, a beach front house in Boca Raton, Florida, and a pre-revolutionary war plantation near Williamsburg, Virginia, called "The Willows." John enjoyed the plantation house more than anywhere in the world. Jenny and he would escape for long weekends to Williamsburg. Of course, John had paid for the installation of high-tech satellite dishes so that he could be wired to the world. John and his wife had so loved the area that it influenced both children to attend and graduate from The College of William and Mary. Both children went to work, married, and started families near Williamsburg.

When John announced his intention of retiring from Smith Goldman about twelve months ago, many enticing offers came his way. He had been offered board directorships on about twenty Fortune 500 companies; he had been offered chairmanships with two public banking establishments; he had even been offered an appointment as a governor of one of the Federal Reserve regions. None of these excited him. John did have one proposal that intrigued him. The College of William and Mary had offered him an opportunity to educate future business leaders in international finance. The course could be an undergraduate or postgraduate course. It was his decision. After many discussions with Jenny, John decided that he was going to take this position and its $120,000 per year salary. John and Jenny could move to The Willows and also be closer to the grandchildren. John had decided he would be willing to teach a course on international finance if the college allowed him to teach a class on capitalism. After the work day ended, Jenny and John were going to board the company's Gulfstream V and fly to Williamsburg. Eventually, they would move full-time to The Willows.

Chapter 2

John awoke at four thirty a.m. as usual. It was a cold December morning, and the covers were keeping him warm. He thought to himself that it was going to be hard to break the habit of waking this early. At five, John finally arose from bed and started his workout. At The Willows, he had installed a state-of-the-art fitness center. The room had several televisions so he could watch multiple news shows simultaneously. After jogging on the treadmill for about thirty minutes, John lifted weights, and then took a shower. By six thirty, he was ready to leave The Willows. However, his meeting with the president of the college was not until eight thirty. John read the *Wall Street Journal* and had a couple of cups of coffee as he waited.

Jenny and John had been extremely generous donors to the college. They had funded three individual scholarships and had given a $25 million donation to the endowment. Once every year, the president of the college, Doctor Thornton Smith, invited Jenny and John to his house for cocktails and dinner. At this dinner, Smith would bring the couple "up to speed" on the situation at the college and ask them for a donation to answer any specific needs. Over the years, checks of $10,000 to $50,000 could be expected at the conclusion of the dinner.

When it became news that John was going to be leaving Smith Goldman, Smith called John and offered him a teaching position at the business school. In the beginning, John thanked the president for the gracious offer. But as time wore on, John began feeling a sense of duty to take time and pass along the knowledge that he had gathered during his thirty-year career. In September 2010, during the annual president's dinner, Smith talked at length about the offer and what it would entail. After the discussion, John told Smith that he would talk it over with Jenny and get back to him shortly. A couple of days before Thanksgiving, John telephoned and formally accepted the position. At the conclusion of the call, it was decided that John would visit Smith on December 3rd, two days after his last day at Smith Goldman.

Finally, it was eight a.m. and John left The Willows for the college. The meeting was going to be held in the president's house, which is just to the right as one faces the J. Christopher Wren Building while standing on the Duke of Gloucester street. John pulled his 2011 Ford F-150 pickup into the parking lot behind the President's House and walked around to the front door. As he balled up his fist to knock, the front door opened with a very toothy Doctor Smith eagerly meeting him. He welcomed John through the front door, and they went to the study and sat down.

After a few minutes of pleasantries, Smith thanked John for agreeing to come to William and Mary and for teaching the future leaders of the country. Accordingly, John thanked Smith for the wonderful opportunity. Based on past negotiation experiences, John knew that any changes in the agreement had to be discussed in the first ten minutes of the meeting. He stated he was excited about teaching the graduate-level business course but wanted to discuss another idea. John started laying out his plan of teaching a course on capitalism and the free-market system. He continued by discussing how he would

5

look at the events from 1994 until the 2008 financial meltdown and what caused it. He also wanted to discuss the steps that had been taken since then by the Obama administration and how those policies were the wrong course of action. Finally, he wanted to discuss ObamaCare and why it was the wrong thing for America.

The College of William and Mary is one the top academic schools in the United States. It is the second oldest college in the country and is well known for its academic prowess. William and Mary, however, is a liberal arts college. Its political affiliation, as with most colleges and universities, is decidedly liberal. This political leaning is largely influenced by the political affiliations of its professors. Therefore, Smith was stunned by the new request. He knew that a class of this subject matter would more than likely be tremendously different from anything taught by the current business school or anywhere else at the college. After a lengthy discussion, Smith asked John for the topics on the proposed course. John had already prepared a course curriculum and required reading list:

Capitalism and the Free Market

Session 1 – History of Capitalism and the Free Market (Part 1)
Session 2 – History of Capitalism and the Free Market (Part 2)
Session 3 - History of Progressivism and its Impacts on the Free Market (Part 1)
Session 4 – History of Progressivism and its Impacts on the Free Market (Part 2)
Session 5 – The Great Depression and Its Impact on the US Economy
Session 6 – World War II and the Aftermath Impact on the Free Market

Smith took the material, promised to study in detail, and get back to John by the end of the week. The two men stood, shook hands, and departed with mutual respect and anticipation of things to come.

Chapter 3

Doctor Smith had spent considerable time studying the curriculum John provided. He was sensitive to both the current faculty, who would more than likely have some issues with this course, and to an exceedingly generous benefactor of the college. Smith felt it was necessary to discuss the matter informally with several of the department chairs, including those in economics, business, and government. The meeting was scheduled for Wednesday afternoon at one thirty. He chose not to alert the group to the subject before the meeting.

Precisely at one thirty, Smith welcomed Dr. Joseph Miller, chairman of the department economics, Dr. Philip Stowell, dean of the business school, and Dr. William Randolph, chairman of the department government. Smith passed out a copy of the course curriculum. After a few minutes, Miller asked, "Are you serious?" Stowell asked if this course was better suited for government versus the business school. Randolph remained silent as the discussion became quite lively.

After almost two hours of lively conversation, Smith thanked each of the department heads for their contribution to the discussion. He asked if he could have a word with Randolph alone. After Miller and Stowell departed, Smith commented that he had noticed that Randolph was quiet during the two-hour discussion. Smith asked Randolph his opinion of the course.

Randolph collected his words carefully and stated, "My opinion is of little importance on this matter. While I am sure that I disagree with the point of view of the instructor, I would say that his opinion should be heard even if it is just opinion."

Randolph had worked with Smith for more than ten years and knew the decision had already been made. This new course was going to be part of the spring semester. He decided he was going to visit the lecture on the first day to see what was discussed. If need be, he would "correct" any misstatements by the former businessman.

Chapter 4

William Randolph had just finished his workout and was getting a shower and dressing for work. William and his wife Sarah had lived in Williamsburg for about twenty-eight years. Their three children had all graduated from William and Mary and had started families in Virginia—two in Northern Virginia and one in a small town in southern Virginia called South Hill.

William was not only the department chairman for the school of government, he was also a chancellor professor at the college. William had received his undergraduate degree from William and Mary in 1978 and received his doctorate in political economy and government from the John F. Kennedy School of Government at Harvard in 1983. He was awarded tenure in 1989 and promoted to professor in 1991. William had written several papers about Keynesian economics, including a doctoral dissertation on its influence on the US economy. William had provided political commentary to the major television networks about the economy. Since the 2007–08 financial meltdown, William had been on the television networks at least thirty times. Since Barack Obama won the presidency, William had been summoned to the White House on two occasions to advise the president.

In the early 1990s, William successfully ran as a Democrat for school board of New Kent County and was reelected. In 1998, he was elected to the Virginia House of Delegates for the county of New Kent. Since 1998, he was re-elected three times. In the 2008 Virginia elections, he was appointed the Democratic state party chairman, and he personally campaigned with Senator Barack Obama. William was more than excited in November 2008 when Senator Obama became President Obama. He was a guest of NBC when Chris Matthews made his infamous comment, "I felt this thrill going up my leg" during the primaries. After the campaign and during 2009, William decided not to run again for the House of Delegates so that he could focus more time on being a husband and faculty member.

William and his wife lived in a nice two-story home within the city of Williamsburg. They were never big-spenders, but they had purchased a lakefront home on Lake Gaston in southern Virginia about twelve years ago. They visited the lake house as often as possible, but it was never enough. William enjoyed navigating the large lake in his twenty-five foot pontoon boat. Eventually, they hoped to retire there for a life of leisure on the lake.

Since stepping down from the Virginia House of Delegates, William decided to take on more classes starting with the spring semester. He would continue teaching the graduate courses on political and economic issues and the role of Keynesian economics. William also decided to teach an undergraduate course. He felt this task would give him an understanding of where the new generation of incoming students was situated from a political point of view.

Today was the first day of the new spring semester, and William's first class was at ten a.m. in Morton Hall, room 312. It was the first time since 1996 that William had taught a 100-level course, and he was a little anxious. He arrived at his office at nine a.m. and reviewed e-mail. At ten, he left his office and entered the lecture hall filled with second-semester freshmen who were ready to learn about economic political science 102.

Chapter 5

John arrived to the first class of "Capitalism and the Free Market" at a little before nine thirty a.m. on Tuesday. The course was held in the largest conference room in Tyler Hall, the undergraduate business school building. It had been scheduled as a Tuesday-Thursday course of one and a half hours long. The conference room was about three-fourths filled with more students filing in every couple of seconds. John was not terribly nervous speaking in front of groups. This group of around fifty was small in comparison of thousands to which he had spoken during his life. He did feel anxious about "teaching" for the first time. He went up to the front of the room and took out his prepared materials and neatly arranged them on the table. He looked up and saw "frightfully young-looking" people. Most were dressed in sweat suits, and their hair was disheveled. There was quite a bit of laughing and talking. John also recognized a familiar face in the back of the room. It was William Randolph. John had known Randolph for many years. He was very curious as to why Randolph was in the lecture hall. John decided he would wait until the end of the class to talk with Randolph.

John asked all students please find a seat so that the discussion could begin. When quiet, he introduced himself and commented on his past work experiences. He discussed the curriculum of the course and passed out a syllabus, which contained a calendar of events, expectations for the course, and a list of materials that should be reviewed before each class session. He told the class that he wanted active and vivacious discussion, and 15 percent of the overall grade would come from class participation. Finally, he stated that the PowerPoint presentation would be on his personal webpage one day before class.

John stated that the first couple of sessions would include discussions on capitalism and the free market. This was the first slide discussed:

Capitalism and the Free Market

Session 1

Capitalism – economic system in which the means of production are privately owned and operated for profit. Income in a Capitalist system is split between the business owners and the workers, but not equally since the owners have more risk.

Capitalism – developed incrementally from the 16th century in Europe. It became dominant in Western world following the demise of feudalism.

Capitalism provided a means of industrialization throughout much of the world.

True capitalism involves three primary things:

a. Privately held

b. Free market

c. Direct relationship between owner and worker

John asked the class their thoughts about the definition of capitalism, in particular the phrase "income in a capitalist system is split between the business owner and the workers, but not equally since the owners have more risk." Most students believed that the owners and the workers should equally share the income. One student used as an example the NFL and the current collective bargaining agreement. John told the story of the chicken and the pig. Both are certainly needed for a good breakfast.

14

However, the pig is more committed. The students' puzzled looks showed that a further explanation was needed. John explained that both are equally needed for breakfast. However, the pig must die to become the bacon while the chicken can continue to produce eggs for someone else's breakfast. The pig is committed to becoming breakfast. This analogy is the same for the owner and the worker. The owner puts his or her money into the venture. Typically they work many more hours and invest their blood, sweat, and tears into the business. If the business fails, the worker can simply walk away while the owner loses his money. That is why the owner's risk is higher, and John argued that the owner should have a bigger piece of the pie.

John also discussed the NFL labor dispute. First and foremost, the negotiation was a mugging. The players did not want 50 percent of the profits; they wanted more than 50 percent of the revenues before the costs of running the business were deducted. John stated that unions are one of the most heinous deterrents to capitalism and the growth of the free market. John knew that he had hit a bit of a nerve with that comment, especially when he looked at the face of William Randolph. John stated the class would discuss unions in more detail later in the course.

The next question that John asked was related to the three things that true capitalism includes. Most agreed that capitalism requires companies that are privately held, but many students believed that, in some cases, state-controlled corporations provide better results for consumers. Finally, there was the issue of direct relationships between owners and workers. Most of the class thought that a direct relationship between the owners and the workers was best. John stated that he wanted the class to consider new ideas and thoughts. He hoped that future classes would help them come to some conviction in their thoughts about all three things making up true capitalism.

Main Types of Capitalism

Session 1

a. **Anarcho-capitalism** – libertarian and individualist anarchist political philosophy advocating the elimination of the state, courts and private defense agencies would mitigate disputes.

b. **Mercantilism** – nationalist-oriented form of early capitalism that uses the state to advance national business interests abroad and based on wealth of nation is based on positive balance of trade with other nations.

c. **Free-market capitalism** – free market consists of free-price system where supply/demand are allowed to reach their equilibrium without intervention from the government. Only role of government is to protect property rights.

d. **Social market capitalism** – a nominally free-market system whereby government intervention is kept to a minimum, but the state provides for social security, unemployment benefits and recognition of labor rights though national collective bargaining schemes.

e. **State capitalism** – state owned of profit seeking enterprises.

f. **Corporate capitalism** – free or mixed market characterized by the dominance of bureaucratic corporations which are legally required to pursue profits. Typically involves schemes to avoid competition.

g. **Mixed economy** – combinations of any two of these.

John's second slide listed the main types of capitalism. After discussing each type, John asked the students which one best describes the United States. Most chose social market capitalism. John stated that the United States is more of a mixed economy; social market capitalism is not the only answer because of the massive government intervention in the system. John further explained the government controls trade by setting tariff rates; the government controls profitability by allowing favorable taxation policies, governmental subsidies, and wage controls; the government confiscates up to 40 percent of all profits of private-held companies through income taxes; the government tells companies who they can hire, and the list continues. John noted Randolph's facial expression and realized that this was another sore subject.

John stated that the subject at the next session would be criticisms of capitalism. The students noisily stood, gathered their belongings, and left the room. John looked up at the back of the room and noticed that Randolph had already left out of the back door. There might be another opportunity to discuss why Randolph had joined the class.

Chapter 6

Thursday morning came terribly early. As John left The Willows, he noticed that when the sun is blocking your visibility it is a hindrance. However, when the sun allows us to see how beautiful the earth is, it is a blessing. John did not know why he was thinking about that today, but he continued to reflect on it all the way to work.

John had all of his materials with him, so he went directly to the auditorium for class. The subject matter of the day was criticisms of capitalism. The first slide consisted of:

Criticisms of Capitalism

Session 2

1. Unfair distribution of wealth and power

2. Tendency to drive toward monopolies

3. Economic and cultural exploitation

4. Repression of workers and of unions

5. Social alienation

6. Unemployment

7. Economic Instability

John noticed as most of the students entered, they were talking and discussing different topics. He also noticed a couple of students talking about the course. He tried to listen, but their conversations were too low. John looked in the back of the room and noticed that Randolph had already joined the class and was settling in for the discussion. Time to start, because it was nine thirty a.m. sharp.

The first question that John asked was if the students believe there was an unfair distribution of wealth and power in this country. There was an immediate discussion on the subject; however, the subject was more on redistribution. John figured that all of the current discussion about redistribution of wealth in the media had enlightened the class. After a more directed discussion, he asked for a show of hands of how many believe there is an unfair distribution of wealth. About 50 percent of the hands went up. John asked those students if everyone having the same amount would be fair. The students overwhelmingly indicated no. The reasoning behind their answer that was that some people work harder, some people have college educations, and some have rich parents. The students were asked what the fairest division of income was based on their previous response. Their answers ranged from the belief that everyone should have the same amount to no one should have more than $200,000. John explained to the students that the current distribution of wealth was based on a lot of things— inheritance, the right profession, and so forth. Critics of capitalism often claim that it too richly rewards the owners and the leaders of businesses and poorly treats the workers. While it is true that the rich have a high percentage of the total wealth in the country, only around 40 percent has come from "newly rich" people. The balance is due to inheritance. As the stock market increases, the percentage of the wealth grows because the "rich" own most of the stock. Conversely, when the market goes down (such as in 2008), the wealth distribution changes dramatically. Therefore, does capitalism create an unfair distribution of wealth? John's conclusion was that the current system favors those who work the hardest and have the greatest opportunities. This statement caused the first "evil-eye" from Randolph as the students seemed receptive to what they were hearing. Liberals find it hard to believe that peoples' success is tied to hard work; instead, the success was created by those people cheating, stealing, and taking advantage of others.

John asked if capitalism drives us toward monopolies. The students were unsure about this question. John stated that the Clayton Act, the Sherman Act, and the Securities Act prevent companies from getting too monopolistic. John did point out that in only one instance was a group excluded from the provisions of anti-monopolistic laws. Before John stated the answer, he looked directly at Randolph and stated the truth that unions were exempt from the provisions of these laws. Evil stare number two.

John led the class through the remaining items on the slide. At the conclusion of the slide, John stated capitalism by itself did not cause any one of these items. Randolph went from an evil-eye to fidgeting.

In another slide, John discussed who the critics of capitalism were:

```
  ┌─────────────────────────────────────────────────┐
  │                  Critics of Capitalism            │
  │                      Session 2                     │
  │                                                    │
  │   1. Socialists                                    │
  │                                                    │
  │   2. Anarchists                                    │
  │                                                    │
  │   3. Communists                                    │
  │                                                    │
  │   4. Social Democrats (Progressives)              │
  │                                                    │
  │   5. Nationalists                                  │
  │                                                    │
  │   6. Some Religions                                │
  │                                                    │
  │   7. Environmentalists                             │
  │                                                    │
  │                                                    │
  │                                                    │
  └─────────────────────────────────────────────────┘
```

John asked the students who socialists are. There were no immediate answers from the students. Socialists are people that advocate the vesting of ownership and control of the means of production and distribution, of capital, land, and so forth, in the community as a whole. Individual ownership and liberty is of second consequence, if of any. Anarchists are people who seek to overturn by violence all constituted forms and institutions of society and government with no purpose of establishing anything in its place. Communists believe that all economic and social activity should be controlled by a totalitarian state dominated by a single and self-perpetuating political party. Progressives or social democrats, by definition, are people who want to make changes. John pointed out that this definition does not reflect the 2011 Democratic Party. Randolph again showed the evil eye. John continued stating that nationalists believe in asserting the nation's interest before other interests. Some religions believe it is sinful to lend and borrow money and to make a profit. Finally, environmentalists believe the environment comes first, no matter the cost or detriment to society.

John asked the students for their thoughts on why these groups of people criticize capitalism and the free market system. The answers ranged from political to fairness. John explained the real reason for criticisms has to do with liberty. Liberty allows each person to reap what they sow. It also allows each person to sell at their own price. Individuals or governments do not set prices; the market sets prices based on supply and demand. John admitted there may be some who cheat or take advantage of the system. Should the entire system be shuttered because of the sins of a few? John noticed that the evil eye had escalated into a reddened face and a crouched sitting position.

John and the students continued to discuss the concept of capitalism and liberty. John was impressed with the dialogue. He asked the students to prepare a short narrative on their position on the fairest means of a society, and then he dismissed them. He immediately tried to make his way through the mass, but when arriving at the top of the stairs, he could see that Randolph had escaped out of the back doors. Another missed opportunity.

John went to his office to answer e-mail and return any missed telephone calls. He tried to telephone Randolph, but there was no answer. Sooner or later, John wanted to ask Randolph his motivation for being in the classroom. Obviously, they would not talk today.

Suddenly, John was startled by a knock on his opened door. He recognized the young man as one of his students from the capitalism class. This student, Jerry, said he was enjoying the class. He was a second year business major, and he also wanted to minor in economics. He told John that he was taking a class in economics this semester under Dr. Randolph, who was explaining the concepts of supply and demand when a comment was made that perplexed him. Jerry further revealed that Randolph stated that a true free market system would not work for the primary reason of people's greed. Greed has required the government to create regulations. Greed has made certain people reliant on the government for support. The free market system by definition could not work in today's society.

John responded to the revelations by voicing his thoughts that greed has negatively impacted the US business world, but it has also had some benefits. The greed of earning more money took the United States from whale oil to crude oil. Greed allowed the creation of fast computers, and allowed businesses to expand and hire new workers. Greed has allowed Japanese car manufacturers to build their cars in the United States. John stated that regulations have done more harm to the free market system that greed ever has. For example in the 1990s, Chinese steel manufacturers started dumping steel into the United States at prices much lower than US manufacturers could produce it. Instead of US manufacturers finding a way to lower the cost of their products, they sent their lobbyists to Congress to impose astronomically high tariffs. This action caused inflation for any products that used steel as a raw material. John stated the US corporate income tax rate of 35 percent is the highest among the G20. There are hundreds of similar stories about how government has done more harm than good to the US economy. After thirty minutes of discussion, Jerry thanked John for his thoughts and left the office.

A weekly newspaper called "The Flat Hat" covers the happenings at the college. That Friday a front-page story appeared with the headline:

The College Hires a Republican Businessman to Teach Capitalism

The article described John as an alumnus, a former CEO of a major investment banking firm, and a large contributor to the college. After reading the article, John was surprised why the writer referred to him as a Republican, as the headline stated. Overall, a pretty harmless article, John thought.

Chapter 7

John arrived at the college on Tuesday at about nine a.m. and went to his office to review e-mail. At about nine-twenty, he walked down the stairs to the main conference hall in Tyler Hall for class. There were about twenty-five students already there, and others were filing in quickly. John was a little apprehensive about today's subject matter, which was titled "History of Progressivism and Its Impacts on the Free Market." He noticed that Randolph was absent today.

History of Progressivism

Session 1

- Started later part of 19th and first part of 20th centuries
- In response to industrialization and in contrast to conservatism movement
- Dealt with government's involvement in social and economic matters
- Progressive movement was considered "socialism-lite"
- Presidents identified with progressive movement – Theodore Roosevelt, Woodrow Wilson, Franklin Roosevelt, Lyndon Johnson
- Heavily supported by unions, both public and private
- My view – the purpose of the government is to balance the unequal social and economic situation of society.

John asked the class who thought of themselves as a progressive. A few students raised their hands. John's second question was who considered themselves a Democrat. More than half of the students raised their hands. Then he asked who considers themselves a Republican, and about 30 percent of the students raised their hands. The final question was: who was not sure of their political affiliation? That finished off the class.

John told them to remember back to their SAT testing and the word analogies. Fill in the blanks:

Progressivism is to Democrats as _____ *is to Republicans.*

Most of the class answered "conservatism." John followed up with:

Progressivism is to socialism as conservatism is to _____ *.*

There were a few answers, but none of them were what John wanted. John answered that progressivism is to socialism as conservatism is to democracy. There were a lot of blank stares in the room. He followed up with a discussion on the theory of conservatism. Thomas Jefferson called himself a member of the Democratic Republican party. Its central tenets were a small central government and for power to reside with the states. James C. Calhoun, vice president for both John Quincy Adams and Andrew Jackson, strongly opposed the buildup of the federal government. Most people during the early years of the United States were either for massive federal government (central power) or limited federal powers (states' rights). The War Between the States settled the matter, and since then, the federal government has continued to expand exponentially. John stated he believed that if one gives someone a right, one must infringe on someone else's.

The second slide showed the following:

Proponents of Progressivism

Theodore Roosevelt	Enforcement of Sherman Act, Trust Buster, Mine Workers Revolt in 1902, massive national parks
Woodrow Wilson	Federal Reserve Act, Clayton Anti-Trust Act, Federal Trade Commission Act, Federal Farm Loan Act, Progressive Income Tax, League of Nations,
Franklin Roosevelt	New Deal Programs, Massive Deficit Spending, Tax Rates of 90%, Federal Deposit Insurance Corporation, Social Security, National Labor Relations Act
Lyndon Johnson	Medicare/Medicaid Acts, Great Society programs, War on Poverty
Barack Obama	ObamaCare, Carbon Taxes, Expansion of Union Rights

John stated that most of the students should know the majority of these presidents and the majority of these programs and acts supported by them. He pointed out that all of these had negative impacts on the economy and most "gave rights" to certain people while "limiting or removing rights" of others.

He pointed out that the Sherman Act of 1890 was enacted over the ten years before Theodore Roosevelt became president; however, he was the first president to enforce the law. Who won? Small companies who were in direct competition with Standard Oil. Who lost? Standard Oil, its stockholders and customers who had to pay higher prices lost. In the mine workers revolt of 1902, Roosevelt forced the workers back to work, and forced the owners to pay considerably more money to the workers. Who won? The workers. Who lost? The owners of this company and other companies (it created a floor on wages).

On Woodrow Wilson, John explained the Federal Reserve Act recreated the central bank. This is the same central bank that Andrew Jackson got rid of eighty years beforehand. This is the same organization that allowed Freddie Mac and Fannie Mae to be created. Who won? Probably no one. Who lost? The whole country. Wilson was also the first to create a progressive income tax. Who won? Lower or no-income individuals. Who lost? Higher income individuals and the economy in general, as more money was needed to fund the federal government, as opposed to creating jobs.

On Franklin Roosevelt, John called Social Security the largest Ponzi scheme in the history of the world. Several students stated that their grandparents would not make it without Social Security. John asked them if their grandparents would have made another way if they knew there was not an entitlement program awaiting them. Who won? No one. It forced the American people not to save but to rely on the federal government. The National Labor Relations Act allowed collective bargaining (thus making unions not subject to the Sherman and Clayton Acts). Who won? In the beginning, the unions won. In the end, China and India won.

On Lyndon Johnson, John's view was Medicare and Medicaid caused massive waste in the nation's medical system. It also allowed for a large redistribution of wealth; the government only pays what it deems to be fair. This forces doctors to charge private insurance companies higher costs. Who won? In the short-term, the people without insurance won. In the long-term, no-one won because of the massive waste and fraud in the system.

On Barack Obama, John explained that ObamaCare was the most reckless, most dangerous entitlement program ever passed by progressives; it was the Holy Grail for them. Every progressive president since FDR has tried to get this passed.

The class was perfectly silent. John knew he had gone against everything that society teaches about some of these presidents. Theodore Roosevelt and Franklin Roosevelt have been consistently rated as two of the best presidents of all times. John's point was that each of these president's policies has negatively impacted the US economy and the free market. Some of the students asked questions and brought up "facts" that they had been "taught" in their prior life. John refuted each one. After the discussion, he dismissed the students. He stated the discussion on the free market system would continue in the next session.

As John left the campus that night, he thought back to how in-shock the students were. It was probably the first time in their lives that they heard anyone say something negatively against FDR and Theodore Roosevelt. He also wondered if those who were taking government or economics courses would discuss the subject with those respective professors. He did not worry, because he had spoken the truth. He was more concerned about what untruths he would need to address. John told Jenny about the class, and she was also concerned about the potential ramifications.

Chapter 8

John was still thinking about Tuesday's class when he walked into Tyler Hall. He still remembered the faces of the students as he had "burst their idealistic bubbles." John knew FDR was probably the worst president in the US history. He also knew World War II was the reason America was able to escape the Great Depressions/Recessions of the 1930s. John walked into the lecture hall at about nine thirty on this cold Thursday morning and noticed Randolph back in his regular chair. Anticipation hung over the classroom.

John started by asking the students if they had any questions or comments from the last class. Immediately the class became a "free for all" as the FDR presidency was further examined. The students brought up:

1. FDR getting the United States out of the Great Depression.
2. FDR's handling of Japan.
3. FDR providing security for the failed banking system.

John refuted each of these (FDR's programs caused massive deficit spending; FDR did not want to go to war but the Japanese forced his hand; the FDIC was a risk transfer from the people who had money in the bank to the taxpayer). The discussion went on about forty-five minutes. John's opinion of FDR was of an egomaniac socialist who had been born into privilege and had never suffered a day of his life. John pointed out this was his opinion, and each student would have to form their own opinion. However, it was crucial they had more points of view than the less-than-factual views to which they were exposed in their precollege education.

John brought up the following power point slide.

Free Market vs. The Controlled Market

Free Market – no economic intervention and regulation by the state, except to enforce taxes, private contracts and the ownership of property.

Controlled Market – the state regulates how goods, services, and labor may be used, priced, or distributed rather than relying on the mechanism of private ownership.

Purposes of the Federal Government

Constitution – enumerated powers spelled out.

Not included – healthcare for everyone, social security, fair trade/anti-trust, progressive tax system (it says fair system)

Big Federal Government XXXXXX Free Market Economy

John asked the students what in their opinion the US economy was based on the definitions in the slide. The students collectively agreed that it was between a free-market and a controlled-market economy. John asked if a woman could be 50 percent pregnant. The class laughed and stated no. John went on to say that either one has a free market economy or one does not. There are no shades of gray. The US economy is a highly controlled market economy. The US economy is controlled by the Department of Justice (Securities and Exchange Commission), the Department of Commerce (Federal

Trade Commission and the Patent and Trademark Office), the Department of the Treasury (Internal Revenue Service), and the Department of Homeland Security (Customs and Border Control). While not as controlled as tightly as a communist government, like China, it is highly controlled, and the economy is vastly limited on its true potential.

John finally asked if it was right for the federal government to have all of these controls when the Constitution does not specifically provide for them. About half the students said yes. They collectively thought that the federal government should protect individuals. John asked those who did not agree to express their thoughts. Collectively, they thought government controlled too much but did see some things that necessary safeguards, such as the Securities and Exchange Commission and the Internal Revenue Service. John told the students that they needed to decide for themselves. He shared his opinion that any power not enumerated in the Constitution was an unlawful power grab by the federal government. He noted that both Democrats and Republicans had overstepped their authority. John also explained the Constitution was abundantly clear that any power not expressly enumerated in this document should fall on the states, as stated in the Tenth Amendment to the Constitution.

John thanked the class for the discussion and said the Great Depression and its impacts on the economy would be discussed in the next session.

Chapter 9

As John drove home that evening, he replayed the discussion in class that day. He was proud of the students for taking the time to think outside of class, as opposed to simply studying the material and regurgitating it for a test.

The next day, John went to the Golden Horseshoe Golf Course in Williamsburg, which is just off of Duke of Gloucester Street. As he pulled into the parking lot, John recognized William Randolph, who was busily putting on his shoes while sitting on the back of his car. John pulled his truck into an empty parking space and quickly walked over to Randolph. Finally, he would find out why the professor had been visiting his class.

"William!" he yelled across the parking lot. John was almost running so that he could catch up to him. He noticed that William had turned around and watched as John hurried toward him. John finally reached him and shook his hand like he had many, many times before.

"Hi, John, how's it going?" William asked. They shared pleasantries and asked about each other's families.

"Hey, glad to have you in my class. Have you found it worth your time to attend?" John asked.

William said that he had to tee off in a couple of minutes but wanted to talk later at the clubhouse after the round.

John watched as William hurried off to join his group for a round of golf. John noticed that his son was pulling into the parking lot. They would have a couple of minutes to loosen up at the driving range before the round. He truly enjoyed playing golf with his son, and was anxious to start the round.

As the round ended, John started thinking about his impending conversation with Randolph. Finally, he would understand why Randolph had been so frequently visiting his class. After finishing the eighteenth hole, John walked inside the clubhouse to visit with Randolph. He had started to think about the future conversation since finishing the ninth hole, so his scoring on the back nine had been poor. His son had won the round, which he had been doing for the last several years.

John walked into the clubhouse and searched for Randolph but did not see him anywhere. John quickly walked to the parking lot and noticed that Randolph's car was gone from its original parking spot. John could not believe that Randolph had departed without talking to him first.

John went back into the clubhouse to find his son. He invited him and his entire family over for barbeque that night. They hugged and departed together. As John drove home, he allowed himself get highly irritated about Randolph's quick departure. John decided to call him tomorrow to confront him for leaving so quickly.

Chapter 10

John and Jenny had been visiting the Baptist church on Richmond Road in Williamsburg. They had talked about joining the church but had not found the right weekend to do so. During the service that morning, John had been stewing about the incident from the previous day and wanted to call Randolph about his rudeness. At the conclusion of the service, Jenny, John, the children, and the grandchildren went to lunch at the Cheese Shoppe, a local restaurant. As usual, John picked up the tab, which he always did for the family. John and Jenny enjoyed the time with the family, in particular after church on Sunday. The grandchildren had been putting pressure on John and Jenny about going to Aspen, Colorado, for spring break so they could ski. Jenny had already decided the answer was yes. John did not know if he could work it into his schedule. As they left the restaurant, Jenny invited the grandchildren over to The Willows to play. As they left, John and Jenny had all of the grandchildren in the F-150 Ford pickup, which was getting to be a normal routine on Sundays.

When they got back to The Willows, the kids ran in the field near the river. Their goal was to visit with the horses. Jenny started yelling at them so that they would not get hurt as they were leaning over a fence. John walked into the house and headed to the master suite. He changed into more comfortable clothes and rode the John Deere Gator down to the horse stable. The kids were feeding the horses hay from the storeroom. John spent the next several hours with the grandchildren as they each took turns riding the horses. This was one of John's true joys.

In a couple of hours, the grandchildren decided to move the fun up to the house. John had installed a movie room in the basement complete with studio chairs. The children decided that they wanted to watch a movie. Jenny had compiled quite a children's movie collection and the kids quickly picked *The Lion King* again. Jenny started the movie and the kids immediately got comfortable. John walked upstairs from the lower level to his office. He had installed an office in The Willows complete with a large desk, book shelves, computers, and large-screen televisions wired into the markets. John wanted to talk with Randolph.

John made the telephone call and Randolph's voice mail picked up. John left a message for Randolph to call him back when he had a chance. He walked downstairs and settled in to watch the rest of the movie with the grandchildren.

Later that night after the children and grandchildren went home, John told Jenny about the entire situation with Randolph. After the discussion, Jenny wisely advised John that he needed to make the time to talk to him as soon as possible but not to worry. John was always amazed at her ability to calm him down from his concerns.

Jenny questioned John about the grandchildren's request for spring break. John said that he would work out his schedule. This surprised Jenny because John had never changed his work schedule in the past. Jenny went to bed elated with anticipation for the big family vacation. John lay awake thinking about the conversation yet to come.

Chapter 11

On Monday as John prepared for class on the next day, he once again thought back to the events from the previous weekend. The golf course incident and the voice mail with no resolution were starting to weight on him. John knew that the discussion for the next class was on the Great Depression and its aftermath. He wondered if Randolph would show for class. He thought back to his days at Smith Goldman and how comparatively easy that was. John spent more time than usual preparing for class because of the distractions. All bases would be covered.

On Tuesday morning, John woke up still thinking about the lack of a response from Randolph. He decided he would walk over to Morton Hall, where Randolph's office was located, after class to confront him. He had been at William and Mary for three weeks without one conversation with Randolph.

John walked into Tyler Hall looking for Randolph. He walked into the main conference room. He noticed that the students were staring at him differently from other sessions. John unloaded his briefcase at the podium at the front of the class and hooked his computer into the overhead projector. He looked up and noticed Randolph had brought a friend, Dr. Joseph Miller, the chairman of the economics department. John felt a nervous twinge in his stomach.

He started out the session with the following PowerPoint presentation:

Session 5 – The Great Depression

I.   What caused the Great Depression?

II. What steps were taken to correct the Great Depression?

III. What worked and didn't work? What were the consequences?

IV. What truly brought the US out of the Great Depression?

V.   Lasting Impacts of the Great Depression?

John asked the class to name the causes of the Great Depression. There were many answers including cheap money causing a massive run up on stocks, large, unsecured debt borrowings, and higher federal spending. John confirmed that all of the above caused the Great Depression including one additional item, which was a true free-market system which will have peaks and valleys— that it is normal. John looked up at both visiting professors for their reactions. Both were uncomfortably fidgeting in their chairs. He continued by explaining that during the "Roaring Twenties," the Federal Reserve, created under President Wilson, completely missed the run up on cheap money and continued to fund the banks at interest rates that were simply too low. The banks were loaning money to people with collateral based on stock valuations. As the market valued decreased, the loans became worthless. John also mentioned President Wilson created several federal programs that provided loans to veterans of World War I that were not based on sound financial principles. Those loans were failing at rates higher than typical failure rates. John also mentioned that Presidents Coolidge and Hoover both failed to identify the impeding market failures and continued on the same path. By October 1929, the US stock market crashed as people tried to liquidate their holdings, with no takers found. The bottom of the Great Depression was not experienced until 1933 when the economy failed, and unemployment approached 25 percent. John explained that the real event that put the US into the depression was the lack of credit available to businesses. Once that was "dried-up," businesses failed. It created a chain-reaction in the entire economy.

The United States was under a complete financial disaster. People were hungry, homeless, and did not know where to turn. Of course, people blamed the government, most importantly President Herbert Hoover. Shanty towns were created all over the country, and the people called them Hoovervilles. While people were in dire straits, President Hoover believed that the economy would straighten out itself without the involvement of the government. Since Hoover did not actively interact, the economy remained in a negative tailspin for the remainder of his presidency. More of John's thoughts to the class:

By the time of the Presidential election of 1932, the people of America were ready for a change in leadership. Franklin Delano Roosevelt, a northern, elitist, rich career politician was elected in a complete landslide. His first action to deal with the Great Depression was to spend massive amounts of money. This action dramatically increased the size of the federal government. His "first 100 days" created the New Deal. The New Deal resulted in the largest expansion of the federal government in this history of the United States. The New Deal created new governmental jobs for the unemployed. In a nutshell, the federal government "borrowed" money from other countries to hire unemployed workers. With the massive deficit spending by FDR during the period from 1933 until 1937, the economy improved. Unfortunately, the massive unfunded spending created a massive recession in 1937.

John asked the class what their thoughts were, so far, based on the lecture. Most of the class stated Coolidge and Hoover caused the Great Depression, and Roosevelt "rescued" America from the Great Depression. John stated the class was totally wrong. The visiting professors both shook their heads in disagreement. John continued by explaining that using debt as a means to fix one problem causes other problems. This was evidenced by the massive recession of 1937. He pointed out that economic recoveries that do not include businesses and employment recovering will eventually fail, as this one did. He told the class that the only thing that brought America out of the financial calamity was World War II.

John asked the class to discuss some of the impacts of the Great Depression. The students mentioned the many government programs created during FDR's Presidency such as Social Security. The students also identified the many new governmental agencies that continue to exist today. John agreed with the comments but wanted some other responses. One of the students mentioned that deficit spending and currency manipulation became a way in which the federal government would combat recessions in the future. He noticed that the visiting professors were frowning at such a comment.

John asked for additional clarification. The student stated the Federal Reserve used spending and interest rates in an attempt to improve the economy. John smiled. That was one of the answers he was hoping the students would identify. John confirmed that the Federal Reserve, and in particularly the governors, had tried to influence the economy since the Great Depression by increasing or decreasing the short-term discount rate—the rate at which the federal government lends to banks. John asked for explanations as to what is wrong with this theory. No one answered. John answered that one of the critical issues of the housing bubble was too much cheap money, which the class would discuss in further detail in a later session. John also stated the creation of massive governmental entities were more than likely unconstitutional. It started a trend of continually adding governmental entities to solve every problem confronting the American people. The recurring theme is once the problem is solved, the governmental entity is not eliminated. Finally, John stated that tax rates went up dramatically. The top-tier rate went to 95 percent—95 percent of the income generated would be taken by the IRS.

The class ended with these final points by John. He mentioned that in the next class that there would be more discussion on World War II and its aftermath. As the students were leaving, John noticed Randolph and Miller walking down the aisle toward the front of the class.

Miller loudly stated, "What you said was not completely the truth."

John answered, "Good morning Doctor Miller and Doctor Randolph. Thank you for joining class today. Perhaps we can adjourn to my office for a discussion."

Both men nodded in agreement and walked out of the classroom in front of John. John thought this could get amusing.

Chapter 12

Once John had offered chairs to both men, Miller stated again that not everything said in John's class was true. John asked which points specifically were not true. Miller began by saying the creation of the Federal Reserve under Wilson was correct, but the people running the Fed when the Great Depression started were appointees of Hoover, a Republican, and the Fed had expanded under Coolidge and Hoover. John agreed with the statement, but pointed out that his statement was the creation of the Federal Reserve, and the setting of federal borrowing rates enabled the banks to lend money backed by fictitious stock valuations. This, in a nutshell, started the chain of events that created the Great Depression.

Miller ignored John's rebuttal and continued that to reverse the course of the worst economic disaster in the country's history was not going to be a quick fix and that John had led some to believe that FDR's policies kept the country in a financial quagmire. John rebutted that FDR's policies did nothing to correct the economy other than putting people to work based on governmental deficit spending. Those programs did not create good, private sector jobs, which every recovery needs. Miller and John continued to make points and counterpoints; however, there would not be an agreement. Finally, Miller remarked that John had been too critical in saying that FDR's creation of new agencies and programs had been unconstitutional. John asked Miller to show him in the Constitution where the federal government should provide Social Security to retirees. Miller stated that it was under the commerce clause of Article 1. John retorted that this was bull, and he knew it. John asked what specifically under Social Security provided interstate commerce. Miller did not have an answer to this question. Miller stated that he would discuss his thoughts about the class with the college president, Doctor Smith, later today as he stormed out of the office.

After Miller left, John looked across at Randolph, who had remained extremely quiet during the entire animated exchange. He asked for Randolph's thoughts. Randolph affirmed that it was his opinion that there were a lot of truths in what was discussed in class. However, he thought that there might have been some factors left out of the discussion. John asked him to provide specific examples. Randolph pointed out that Wilson and FDR were not the first Presidents to be accused of acts that were unconstitutional. Jefferson was accused of unconstitutionally purchasing the Louisiana Purchase in 1803. Lincoln had been accused of overstepping his authority during the Civil War. Grant established the first national park, which was not specifically mentioned in the Constitution. McKinley had been accused of unconstitutional acts during the Spanish-American War. John asked what these events had to do with FDR's presidency. Randolph continued that Wilson and FDR were not the first two Presidents to expand the role of the Presidency. John agreed to this counterpoint. However, John did mention that the power grab by FDR was larger than all of the other combined. Randolph grudgingly agreed.

Randolph and John spent the next two hours talking about several topics discussed in the most recent class, as well as previous classes. In many cases, the men agreed on certain points. There were, however, many points in which there were disagreements. At the end of the two-hour session, Randolph rose from his chair, thanked John for the discussion and warmly shook John's hand. John invited Randolph back to class anytime he wanted and welcomed a repeat of the discussion that they just had. They smiled at each other, and Randolph left the office.

John sat at his desk and thought about the discussion that had just taken place. It was a very intriguing dialogue between Randolph and himself. It always amazed him that two people could have remarkably diverse points of view based on the same fact or circumstance of history. John replayed the discussion several times as he was preparing for the next class.

As John was packing up his computer bag, the telephone rang. John looked at the telephone number on the phone console. He knew that it was a William and Mary telephone number, but he was not sure exactly who it was. John picked up the receiver and quickly learned that it was the president of the college, Thornton Smith. He wanted to know if John could join him for lunch tomorrow in the President's House. John agreed to meet him at noon. After concluding the call, John thought that Miller must have already spoken to the college president. John was looking forward to this conversation. John had always believed that classes at William and Mary, as well as most colleges and universities, were heavily swayed toward a liberal point of view. For the first time, a guest lecturer would be allowed to give a more conservative point of view. John knew this course would be considered "controversial" and exceedingly hard for some to take. John enjoyed playing the role of a rogue, and knew he had made the right decision in proposing and accepting this teaching position. As he walked on the brick sidewalks out to his truck, John was really looking forward to lunch tomorrow.

Chapter 13

John went to his office on Wednesday morning to prepare for Thursday's class. The session was to discuss World War II and its impacts on the free-market system. John believed he would have visiting professors in the session. Of course, which ones would be a surprise.

At around eleven thirty a.m., John decided that he would start his walk to the President's House. The walk from Tyler Hall was not terribly long, but John always liked to walk around the J. Christopher Wren building when going in that direction. He imagined some of the country's founders walking on the same sidewalks. As he was facing Duke of Gloucester Street, he turned left and walked up to the front door of the President's House. John knocked on the door and waited. The door swung open to reveal the toothy smile of Thornton Smith, who invited John into the house. Smith motioned for John to sit down, and he began to explain a conversation that he had the previous day with Doctor Miller. Smith told John that Miller had been extremely irate about the session the day before, and expressed concern that not all of the facts had been presented to the students. John simply nodded as he listened. After about ten minutes, John confirmed he knew Miller had some issues with the materials presented the previous day. However, John pointed out that he used factual material to support his conclusions. John consented that the material might have had a more conservative slant, but he said he would wager that Miller's lectures more than likely had a more liberal slant. John also revealed that Miller had a real issue with John's opinion of FDR being one of the worst presidents in the history of the United States. Smith said that he did not agree with John's opinion either. He continued by saying that FDR typically goes down as one of the best presidents in the history of America. John responded that statement proved his point. John continued to say that people who liked FDR point out Social Security, the leader during World War II, the many new jobs that FDR created, and so forth. Further, his opinion was that FDR was an egomaniac as proven by his running for a third and fourth term, and he did not truly understand what he was doing with Social Security as now the nation is trying to make the program solvent in the future. John continued to explain FDR significantly increased the size of the federal government and increased taxes. John stated that while many liked what FDR did as president, he was not one of them. Smith said he understood and motioned for John to adjourn to the dining room for lunch.

During lunch, the two men continued discussing their differing points of view. Smith stated that he had a better appreciation of the different points of view. At the conclusion of the meal, John thanked Smith for his hospitality and departed.

As he leisurely walked back to his office, he thought about the conversation. While nothing was solved, it was entertaining to "shock" the liberal establishment about their most sacred cows such as FDR.

Chapter 14

John woke up the next morning ready for the new day. There were signs of spring, and that always made John feel mentally and physically energetic. He worked out, had breakfast, showered and was already out the door by seven o'clock. He marveled at the new buds on the trees that lined the road in and out of The Willows.

When John arrived at his office, he noticed the voice-mail light. He entered the keystrokes on the telephone, and there were two voice mails. The first was from Thornton Smith thanking him for lunch the previous day. Smith invited John and his wife to an alumni reception in a couple of weeks. John jotted down the relevant information and deleted the message. The second voice mail was from Joseph Miller, John's sparring partner from the previous day. Sounding contrite, Miller apologized for his less than professional dialogue in John's office from the previous day. He also asked if they could meet to discuss their differing points of view early the next week. John made himself a note and would return the call after class.

John quickly reviewed his material for class that morning. The subject was World War II and its Impact on the American economy. John did not think that this class or its subject matter would be as controversial as the prior session. He looked at his watch and noticed that it was about nine fifteen. It was time to start making his way down to the classroom.

When John walked in, he noticed there were no professors in the back row. As the students were filing into the classroom, he noticed a couple of unfamiliar faces. John did not think too much more about it at that time. He displayed the following slide:

Session 6 – World War II and The US Economy

- In 1940, GDP was $101B and federal spending was $9.47B. Defense spending was $1.66B.
- In 1941, GDP was $120.7B, federal spending was $13B and Defense was $6.1B
- In 1942, GDP was $139.1B, federal spending was $30B, Defense was $22B
- In 1943, GDP was $136B, federal spending was $64B, Defense was $44B
- In 1944, GDP was $175B, federal spending was $73B, Defense was $63B
- In 1945, GDP was $174B, federal spending was $72B, Defense was $65B

What are the parallels?

Source: www.usgovernmentspending.com

John asked the students to discuss their observations from the information on the slide. The class focused on the rapid growth of the economy as evidenced by the GDP. They also noticed the fast growth of defense spending. John wanted the class to notice something else, as he pointed out in 1940, nondefense spending was around $7 billion, and in 1945, the same spending was around $9 billion. The federal government, other than defense, had been held in check.

John asked for an explanation as to what happened to unemployment during World War II. The students were unsure. He told the class that the unemployment rate was 15 percent in 1940 and went down to 1.9 percent by 1945.

The American people mobilized for the war effort. Women began working in factories, which was uncommon prior to the war. John mentioned that not since the early stages of the industrial revolution had the world seen such a massive increase in manufacturing and the almost doubling of the GDP.

John asked if there were any negatives from World War II besides the deaths of so many human beings. He told the class that the national debt increased from $48 billion in June 1941 to $259 billion in June 1945. The United States borrowed more than $200 billion to finance the war effort. When FDR took office in 1933, US debt was $19.5 billion. That is a twelve-year increase of $230 billion. In today's dollars, the figure is not a huge deal. However in 1945, the GDP was only $222 billion. The federal debt was greater than GDP.

"Does this remind you of another time in history?" John asked.

John advanced the PowerPoint presentation to the next slide and asked for any comments:

Session 6 – World War II and The US Economy

- In 1946, GDP was $222B, federal spending $55B, Defense $43B
- In 1947, GDP was $244B, federal spending $35B, Defense $13B
- In 1948, GDP was $269B, federal spending $30B, Defense $9B
- In 1949, GDP was $267B, federal spending $39B, Defense $13B
- In 1950, GDP was $294B, federal spending $43B, Defense $14B

What is significant?

Source: www.usgovernmentspending.com

The students brought up the large decrease in defense spending from 1946 until 1947. They also noticed that the economy was relatively flat from 1946 to 1947 and flat for 1948 and 1949. John pointed out the constant increases in nondefense spending during that time. The spending went from around $7 billion to $9 billion in war time to almost $30 billion by 1950. During this time, the national debt decreased by $1.2 billion. How could this be? John's conclusion: The high tax rate implemented during FDR's presidency was not revoked after the war. The size of the federal government started to increase dramatically during the Truman administration and continued during the Eisenhower administration. During the 1950s, the national debt increased another $29 billion, or around 10 percent.

In conclusion, John asked the class to conclude on what was the most significant thing that came after World

War II. Most of the students correctly identified the increase in nondefense governmental spending. John told the class that once programs and agencies are created, they are impossible to eliminate. This is called the "ratchet" effect. As time passes, spending is continually ratcheted up.

John reminded the students they would have their midterm examination next Thursday and to begin studying. The class concluded.

John walked back to his office and returned the phone call from Thornton Miller. Unfortunately, voice mail picked up immediately. John left a message and included his cell phone number for Miller to return the call. John collected his belongings, powered down his computer, and left for the day. As he got into his truck, he noticed how beautiful the day was. He decided to walk around a while along Duke of Gloucester Street. He thought about the class discussion that day but lost himself in the beauty of Colonial Williamsburg.

Chapter 15

On Friday, John decided to go into his office at the college for a while. John wanted to prepare the lecture material for Tuesday's class. He also wanted to put final touches on the midterm examination, which he started weeks ago. When John logged onto his computer, he noticed *"The Flat Hat"* was already in his e-mail reader. To his surprise, he found the following article in the newspaper's opinion pages:

Professor John Causing Stir at William and Mary

"Professor John," as he likes to be called, is causing quite a stir in the business school and other departments around campus. Professor John's class, called "Capitalism and the Free Market," is examining history from a different point of view than what is taught in the U.S. educational system. Professor John has criticized the presidencies of Woodrow Wilson and Franklin Roosevelt and called them two of the worst presidents in the history of the United States. He has said that entitlement programs were ill-conceived and were particularly serious mistakes at the least. Just in the past week, Professor John was summoned to the office of college President Thornton Smith for a discussion regarding the hoopla.

This point of view should have been expected by President Smith. Professor John was the chief executive officer of Smith Goldman. During his career as the head of Smith Goldman, he received massive salaries and unjustifiable bonuses. His company was one of the companies that received bailouts from President George W. Bush and President Barack Obama. Now Professor John wants to come to our magnificent campus and rewrite history to suit his story. There have been reports that the political science and economics department chairpersons have had to spend valuable time and resources countering the inaccuracies of Professor John.

This course is a right-wing propaganda tool for the Republicans. It is attempting to sway the minds of college students to falsehoods and half-truths discussed in class. His position was probably paid for by the Tea Party, and probably a means to help the Republican Party defeat President Obama in the 2012 election.

It is time for William and Mary students to exercise our free rights as students and citizens. Send e-mails to President Smith and Dr. Philip Stowell, the business school Chairman, to voice your anger at such a biased course being taught at our great educational institution.

John sat there for a minute as his blood thoroughly boiled. He thought back to the last class and the unfamiliar faces that he saw in class. Some of these students were probably on the staff of "*The Flat Hat.*" John could not believe the absolute untruths in the article. It was his understanding staff was monitored by a group of professors. How could these professors allow such unsubstantiated untruths and lies be told?

John thought about writing a response to the article but, after some thinking, decided that responding would be of little value. He was startled when his phone rang and he saw the name of William Randolph. John picked answered, and Randolph was thoroughly irritated. He could not believe the article had been written, and could not believe the untruths in the article. He voiced many sincere apologies. John also received phone calls from Smith and Stowell, who both apologized and said they would get to the bottom of it.

John packed up his computer bag, closed his office door, and started walking toward his truck. He saw many students on the way and wondered how many had read and believed the article. When John got home, he showed a copy of the article to Jenny. She was also extremely angry about the article. They spoke at great length about it over the weekend. John started to wonder why he brought this grief on himself by agreeing to become a guest lecturer. There is no limit to what a progressive will do to move their socialist agenda forward.

Chapter 16

When John got to work on Tuesday, he had more than two hundred e-mails. Prior to becoming a college professor, John would continually stay "wired" to his e-mail through a Blackberry. But when he left "the real world," he decided he would stop that practice. John started to go through the e-mails. Some of them were encouraging, but most were critical of the class that John was teaching. Being a former CEO, John was accustomed to not being popular; however, most of the time the label of "bad guy" had been built on some aspect of the truth. As John read the e-mails, he thought about how "brainwashed" these kids were and how intolerant they were to other points of view. As he moved down the list and became bored, he noticed one from *"The Flat Hat."* John decided to read this one:

To:	JRR@wm.edu
From:	EditorFlatHat@wm.edu
Subject:	Article Appearing In Last Friday's Edition

Dear Professor John,

My name is Bill Johnson, and I am the Editor in Chief of *"The Flat Hat"* newspaper. It has been brought to my attention that the article written about you had many inaccuracies and untruths. The writer and the review staff did not exercise sufficient due care in verifying the comments made. The writer has been permanently suspended, and we are reassessing our processes to ensure this does not happen again.

In this week's edition, a complete retraction will be included on Page 1.

Please accept my sincere apology for any inconveniences that this article may have caused you.

Sincerely,

Bill Johnson
Editor in Chief

John was utterly stunned. Very rarely had John seen someone owning up to a mistake and taking responsibility; never had John seen the press do such. It was shocking, to say the least. John was curious as to what caught the editor's attention causing such a 180-degree change in direction. John decided that he needed to respond to this e-mail:

To:	EditorFlatHat@wm.edu
From:	JRR@wm.edu
Subject:	Re: Article Appearing in Last Friday's Edition

Dear Mr. Johnson,

I accept your apology for the mean spirited and untruthful article written in *"The Flat Hat"* last Friday. I would be interested to know what was brought to your attention that made the article untruthful in your eyes.

I look forward to reading the retraction in the next edition.

Regards,
Professor John

John looked at his watch. It was nine twenty, and he rushed down to the lecture hall. He was running late.

Chapter 17

John walked into the classroom and noticed he had a full house. This was expected since the next class was the midterm examination. He also noticed that William Randolph was back in his usual chair in the back of the lecture hall. John connected his computer to the projector and powered up his laptop. As the computer was starting up, John welcomed the students to the lecture and reminded them about the midterm examination on Thursday. He told them that he would share some points of interest at the end of class.

John presented the following PowerPoint slide:

Session 7 – Kennedy's Death and Future Impacts

- John F. Kennedy was elected in one of the tightest elections in US History
- Kennedy was born to very wealthy parents, his father was Ambassador to Great Britain during the 1930s.
- When Kennedy became President, the economy was in bad shape and world events such as the Bay of Pigs, Cuban Missile Crisis engulfed his administration.
- Kennedy's economic advisors wanted a stimulus plan of $10 billion – Kennedy balked
- In 1963, Kennedy agreed to a reduction in taxes for everyone, closing some loopholes, taking the maximum rate from 91% to 70%, new standard deduction, lower withholdings.
- Kennedy died before the bill was enacted, Johnson signed the bill into law.
- Liberal critics of the bill stated that 54% of the benefits would be received by the top 12% of the tax payers.
- By 1964-65, the economy was growing rapidly. Why? **The Multipiler Effect!**

John spoke about the 1960 presidential election between John F. Kennedy and Richard Nixon. Nixon was the vice president for President Dwight Eisenhower and was expected to easily win the election. The charisma of Kennedy and the massive amount of money spent by the Democratic Party enabled Kennedy to win the closest election in American history at that time. Kennedy was born to Patrick and Rose Kennedy, who were extremely wealthy. John asked if there were any similarities to John Kennedy and Franklin Roosevelt. The students immediately pointed out that both were from extremely wealthy parents. John made the comment that it is sometimes very difficult for the super-rich to truly understand how "regular" people think. John quickly looked at Randolph who was shrugging at this comment. John laughed to himself.

John stated that when Kennedy took office, the US economy was not great. In addition, Kennedy's presidency was hounded by world events—Bay of Pigs, the blockade of Cuba, and the Cold War. His chosen economic advisors, the Keynesian crowd, wanted large stimulus spending to improve the economy. Kennedy balked at this. Eventually Kennedy decided on tax cuts for everyone. His critics stated that 54 percent of the tax benefits would help the top 12 percent of taxpayers. John knew this was a time for a "soap box moment." The reason that 54 percent of the benefits would be for the top 12 percent of taxpayers was the top 12 percent were paying 80 percent of the taxes! Randolph was now shifting in his seat. John continued by saying, at that time, the top tax rate during Kennedy's presidency was 91 percent. It was a wonder the economy grew at all after FDR increased the taxes rates that high.

John asked the students to explain what happened after the tax cuts. The students talked about how the economy started growing again. John asked them to explain. They said that there was more money in the economy, thus more potential for growth. This is called the Multiplier Effect. John showed the following slide:

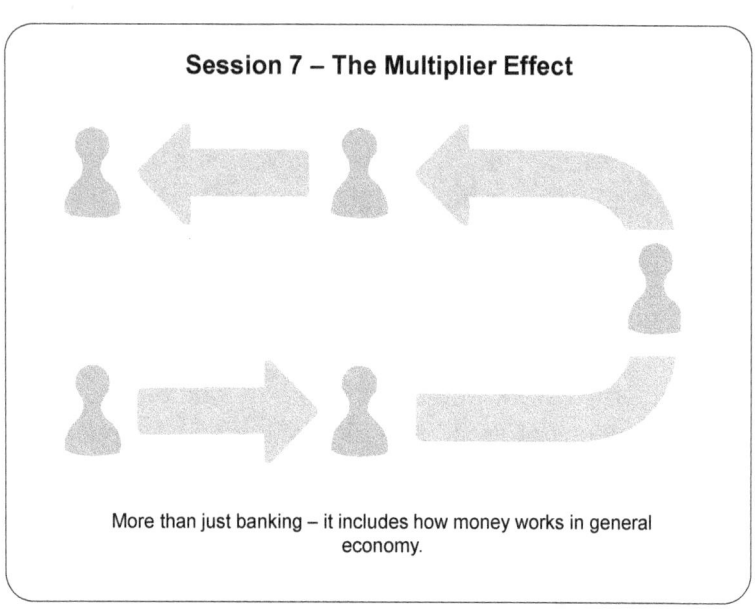

Session 7 – The Multiplier Effect

More than just banking – it includes how money works in general economy.

John explained as one person gets additional money, that person hires or buys something from the next person, and a chain is started. As long as each person continues the cycle, the economy grows. John asked for an explanation as to why this effect does not always work. The students were not able to fully explain, so John continued. When one person in the chain decides to save or is forced to do something else such as paying more taxes, the chain is broken. The concepts of supply and demand have to be considered in this equation.

John showed the class what happened after the economy improved with the following chart:

Session 7 – Kennedy's Death and Future Impacts

- With the economy improved and the country still mourning over the death of a President, Johnson introduced the "Great Society."
- Major programs includes
  a. Civil rights
  b. War on Poverty – food stamps, major changes to social security
  c. Education – Head Start, Teachers Corp
  d. Medicare – first time for publicly funded health care
  e. Medicaid – state run, federal funded
  f. Public Broadcasting – PBS
- At the same time, the war in Vietnam was escalating.
- During Johnson's term, the deficit went from single digit billion to double digit billion
- Both Nixon and Ford expanded many of this programs

John contended that as soon as the economy improved, Johnson took advantage of additional tax revenues and a mourning country and introduced his Great Society. Not since FDR had the government been expanded as much and as rapidly. Some of the programs were beneficial—civil rights. Most, however, were short-sighted. Food stamps, major changes in Social Security, Medicare, Medicaid, and federal funding for public broadcasting were all programs brought forth by the progressive Lyndon Johnson. Some of the other spending initiatives included funding for the arts, Head Start, and the Teachers Corp. There was not a spending opportunity that Johnson could refuse. John asked the students if this reminded them of other presidents. Randolph's eyes were bulging from his face now. In addition to the domestic spending, Johnson also escalated America's involvement in Vietnam. With the additional spending, deficits went from single-digit billion-dollar deficits, to double-digit billion-dollar deficits. John concluded that both Nixon and Ford expanded many of these programs. The ratchet effect proved itself again in all of its glory. John concluded, from a fiscal point of view, Johnson is one of the three worst presidents of all time. His lack of understanding of the future impacts of his massive spending increases and the social programs he enacted were extremely harmful to future generations. This, of course, was contrary to most historians' point of view. Most historians downgrade Johnson because of America's expanded involvement in Vietnam.

John reminded the students of the midterm examination on Thursday and the class concluded. Several students approached him afterward and told him how sorry they were for the article in *"The Flat Hat."* He thanked them for their concerns as they walked out of the classroom together.

As John walked into his office, he noticed that Randolph was sitting in one of the visitor chairs. They greeted one another and started to discuss what John had presented during class. Both Randolph and John enjoyed the discussion, even though neither would fully admit it.

Chapter 18

John walked into his office on Wednesday morning, needing to finish the midterm examination that would be administered tomorrow. As usual, he powered up his computer. He began reading e-mail, and one of them caught his eye:

To: JRR@wm.edu
From: EditorFlatHat@wm.edu
Subject: Re:Re:Article Appearing In Last Friday's Edition

Dear Professor John,

Thank you for accepting my apology.

Unfortunately, I cannot reveal my sources of information. I apologize for this and hope that you understand.

Sincerely,

Bill Johnson
Editor in Chief

This response did not surprise John at all. He continued reading e-mails regarding the article from the previous week until he was bored. At this point, John began working on the upcoming examination.

John decided to evaluate the students over several essay questions. He was not simply looking for canned answers but was interested to see how the students explained and backed up their opinions. He decided on these essay questions:

1.   What caused the Great Depression? Which president contributed most to the Great Depression and why?

2.   Do you agree with the steps that President Roosevelt took to free America from the Great Depression? Why or why not?
3.   Which programs created by President Roosevelt were beneficial for America and which ones were harmful? Discuss the impacts today.
4.   Why was President Johnson able to pass his Great Society agenda?
5.   Which Great Society programs were good for America, and which ones were harmful to America? Please discuss the impacts today.

John was anxious to read the students' responses to these questions. This would be an enjoyable weekend project.

On Thursday morning, he passed out the questions, and the students began filling out their blue books. John was confident most students would take the entire ninety minutes to complete the examination. One student finished in about forty-five minutes; most finished between an hour and an hour and fifteen minutes. Afterward, he collected all of the blue books, shoved them into his computer bag and went home. As John was walking out to his truck he knew he would be anxious to start reading students' responses tomorrow. By the time dinner was served on Thursday night, John had read almost half of them.

Chapter 19

On Friday as John continued reading the blue books, he was impressed, shocked, confused, and underwhelmed. In general, the students had either regurgitated what they thought he would like to hear (or perhaps he had gotten through to them), or they were still caught up in an idealistic world where everyone should be equal (in terms of paychecks, taxes paid, etc.). There were very few opinions and commentaries that were in the middle in blaming both parties.

On one portion of question 1 that asked which president contributed most to the Great Depression, John was fascinated by two different responses. The first one came from a female:

> *In my opinion, the Great Depression was caused by World War I. During the war, the economy contracted as businesses and resources were used in the war effort. When the war was over and the service men came back from overseas, the US economy grew by 42% in the next 10 years (1920–1929). This growth was completely unsustainable as historical growth rates were 3% per year (or no more than 27% during this 10 year period).*
>
> *In addition, during this time period, the federal receipts were in excess of federal expenditures. During this 9 year period, the debt was reduced by $11 billion which represented a 43% reduction in the debt. The Federal Reserve at this time was continuing to lend as much money as it could to banks. When a slight hiccup happened, it started a snowball effect by causing runs on banks, and the banks not being to meet all liquidation requests.*
>
> *Therefore the president who had the most to do with causing the Great Depression was Woodrow Wilson.*

John was extremely impressed with the insight that this student had on this subject. In addition to this response, the following response from a young man floored him:

> The president that had the most to do with causing the Great Depression was Theodore Roosevelt. Roosevelt became President after the assassination and death of William McKinley. Roosevelt was the youngest person ever to hold the office of President at the time, and he ruled the office with an iron fist.
>
> After the completion of McKinley's term and one term of his own, Roosevelt decided to step down. Roosevelt handpicked William Howard Taft as his replacement and expected Taft to continue to do things as he would have. However, Roosevelt soon realized that Taft was "his own man" and made certain decisions that were contrary to Roosevelt. As the election of 1912 approached, Roosevelt ran for the Republican nomination for President against his hand-picked successor. Roosevelt lost the nomination. Acting like a spoiled brat, he formed a third party called the Bull Moose Party and ran against both the incumbent Taft and Democrat nominee Woodrow Wilson. Of course, the Republican vote was split, and Wilson won the election with 42% of the vote.
>
> Woodrow Wilson, who at the time of the election was the president of Princeton University, became president of the United States. Wilson created the Federal Reserve and implemented many progressive programs. Therefore, the person most responsible for creating the Great Depression was Theodore Roosevelt.

John had never thought of Roosevelt causing the Great Depression. However, he began to think what a second term of Howard Taft might have looked like. It was obvious the Federal Reserve would not have been created. Who would have been the Republican successor to Taft?

Wilson was the only Democrat to hold the presidency from 1890 until 1933, but he had never thought that the third party running of Roosevelt caused the Federal Reserve. He was impressed with this student's rationale and thinking.

Of course, John also received some commentaries that were predictable. He quickly calculated that 55 percent of the students thought that Wilson had the biggest impact on creating the Great Depression. Almost 44 percent of the students blamed either presidents Hoover or Coolidge. John graded the papers based on backing up their positions more than agreeing with his positions. He had about ten papers that he thought were exceptional and gave those As. There were three papers written by students who had not properly prepared for the examination and were given Fs.

John was surprised that he finished grading all of the blue books by Friday night. He had assumed he would have weekend homework. He decided to pack-up and go home but decided to check his e-mail one final time. There was an e-mail from *"The Flat Hat"* announcing this week's edition. John decided to open it and read it. The lead article was:

Retraction: Professor John Offered Apology
By The Editor of *The Flat Hat*

Dear Students and Faculty,

In last week's edition of "*The Flat Hat*," the lead article entitled "Professor John Causing a Stir at William and Mary" was found to be riddled with many errors, unfounded accusations, and complete untruths. The writer of the article has been terminated due to using this platform in pushing a political agenda. I have personally apologized to Profession John, and he has graciously accepted the apology. Publicly, I want to apology again for the hurtful, untruthful comments made by the writer and promise all steps are being taken to prevent this type of slander from happening again.

Editor in Chief
The Flat Hat

John felt some vindication by the retraction. He knew that by coming to William and Mary and teaching a course with a nontraditional point of view he was going to cause some waves. He had idealistically hoped that the criticisms would be based on truth and not lies. Of course, he knew that progressives used whatever means necessary to further their agenda. He knew introducing negative comments about Wilson, Roosevelt, and Johnson would be seen as an attack. He decided to let this episode pass. He packed up his computer and went home.

Chapter 20

John awoke at five a.m. to a beautiful spring Saturday morning. He looked forward to that night because the children and grandchildren were coming over for a cookout. John and Jenny had also invited William Randolph and his wife. John had known the couple for many years and appreciated the conversations they'd had over the last couple of weeks.

Whenever John cooked barbeque, he always thought back to the North, where he lived for so many years. In the North, *barbeque* is a verb; in the South, it is a noun. In the north, one would cook a steak on the grill and call it barbeque. Southerners would take pork in the form of shoulders, halves or ribs, slow cook it over wood in a smoker and put barbeque sauce on it at the end of the process. True pit masters would also use a rub on their meat before cooking. John had perfected a homemade rub over the years and would always administer it on any meat put on the smoker. There are many different types of barbeque sauce. In the eastern part of North Carolina, there is a vinegar-based barbeque sauce. In the western part of the state, there is a tomato-based sauce. In South Carolina, the sauce is mustard-based, and in Alabama, a mayonnaise-based sauce is preferred. John loved each and every one of them. The key, though, was the meat. It must be cooked slowly and for a long time.

John walked downstairs and then outside to the pool area. He fired up some charcoal, which he used as a base. He also prepared his wood, which included soaking hickory and a sweet wood such as cherry, maple, or apple.

Today, he was using apple wood. When the charcoal was ready, he poured it into the fire box and put the shoulder into the tower to the right of the fire box. He also put a generous portion of wet wood chips into the fire box. The smoke started rolling out of the smoker—the smell of the South! John would continue putting charcoal and wood chips into the smoker every hour for the next six hours. At around one p.m., John put ribs into the tower. At about five o'clock, the barbeque was ready for consumption.

John had also prepared baked beans, cole slaw, and grilled corn. Jenny had prepared her world-famous banana pudding. The magnificent southern dinner was ready, and now it was time for the guests. John and Jenny had just enough time to change and freshen up before the guests arrived around six o'clock.

Promptly at six, the house came to life with children and grandchildren everywhere. As usual, the grandchildren immediately ran out of the back of the house directly to the pastures on the back of the property. John always got a kick out of watching them run down the field. He greeted the children and invited them into the house. As usual, everyone congregated in the kitchen. This was another colossal difference between the North and the South. In the North, adults congregate in the family room for discussion. In the South, everyone piles into the kitchen. John never truly understood that because the chairs were never as comfortable. It was also typically noisy. Of course, there was always chance that a pre-meal morsel could be enjoyed.

The doorbell rang, and John got up and went to the door. He opened the door and saw a smiling William Randolph and his wife, Sarah. John welcomed them, and they went into the house. John joked with Randolph about some current events as they walked into the kitchen. Jenny hugged both Sarah and William and welcomed them. The adults started into many different conversations about the weather, current events, grandchildren, and many other subjects. Dinner was served around six thirty, and everyone devoured a vast amount of food. After dinner, everyone progressed to the screened porch for dessert and continued fellowship.

The Randolphs left around nine thirty, and the grandchildren stayed for a sleepover. After some television with the grandchildren, John and Jenny finally got to bed around eleven o'clock. They knew it was going to be a tough effort, but everyone was going to church in the morning.

Chapter 21

John arrived at the classroom just in time to start class. He handed out the graded blue books. Most of the students were surprised to get the midterm examinations back so quickly. Students had grown accustomed to getting examinations back in a couple of weeks and surely never at the next class. John commended them on their responses to the examination questions. He shared the two responses that most intrigued him. John invited any student having specific questions on their grade to make an office appointment.

John showed the following PowerPoint slide:

Session 8 – The 1970s and Dependency on Foreign Oil

- End of Vietnam war – from 1969 until 1980, 16 million new workers came into workforce – unemployment went from 3.3% to 8%.
- Policies enacting during the 1960s and a Federal Reserve not interested created very high inflation of up to 14% (Paul Volcker appointed in 1980)
- Stagflation began – high inflation and a recessionary economy
- Major environmental movements began – US and other western countries decided to "save" their oil and start purchasing from the Middle East. Oil imports went from 24% in 1970 to 65% in 1980.
- Yom Kipper War between the Arabs and Israel (Israel won due to western support)
- Due to Israel's victory, the Arab Oil Embargo began. Prices went from $0.35 per gallon to over $1.00 per gallon (they have never returned back to below $0.90 per gallon.
- Nixon taking the US off of the gold standard – due to increased deficit spending
- Nixon/Ford/Carter increased the country's debt by over $500 billion. When Nixon took over, the total debt of the country was $370 billion (1).
- 2000s and the 1970s have been compared (to be discussed later in the course)

(1) - Source: www.usgovernmentspending.com

John explained that the 1970s were a terrible decade economically. The deficit spending caused by the Vietnam War and the costs of the many programs enacted by President Johnson were choking the economy. In addition, the Federal Reserve was totally disinterested in controlling inflation, and let it grow freely during the decade. Not until Paul Volcker was hired did the Federal Reserve start setting monetary policy to reduce inflation. Of course, this abrupt change in monetary policy created the 1981–1982 recession.

John also discussed the concept of "stagflation," which occurs when there is exceptionally high inflation and either a stagnant or recessionary economy. He invited responses on how that could happen in a free market. The students gave a wide array of answers. The answer is that stagflation cannot happen in a true free-market economy. President Nixon's wage and price controls and the impact of the Arab oil embargo caused the stagflation.

John also stated that the environmentalist movement that we know today started in the late 1960s and strengthened during the 1970s. The concept of "running out of oil" began to be discussed, and many western nations hoarded their own oil reserves and bought from Middle East countries. The Environmental Protection Agency started in 1970 and became a cabinet-level agency. It created a massive bureaucracy to limit the amount of oil drilling that could be done. Since it takes years and years for an oil well to produce oil, the United States was caught flat-footed. John pointed out this continues to happen even today and will be discussed further later in the course.

Finally, John wanted to discuss the amount of additional debt taken on during the 1970s. At the start of the decade, US debt was around $370 billion. During the ten-year period, the debt increased by over $500 billion. John pointed out that in the history of the United States, only during wartime did the accumulated deficits of a decade exceed the debt at the beginning of the decade. Beginning with the 1970s, the accumulated deficits for the decade exceeded the debt level at the beginning of the decade, with the exception of the 1990s. John pointed out that the 1990s only made the mark by about $100 billion. John asked for reasons. The students had several answers, but there was only one answer. The size of the federal government has imploded over the last forty years. Military spending has skyrocketed. Entitlement payments have exploded. Governmental bureaucracies have emerged everywhere. The federal government has expanded to a point of no return. When President Bill Clinton said the budget was balanced, this was a lie. The deficit was more than $60 billion in 2000.

John concluded that the government and the American people failed to learn from the mistakes of the 1970s. Massive and uncontrolled spending and dependency on foreign oil were the biggest tragedies of the 1970s.

John told the class that the next session would be about the greatest decade of prosperity since the 1800s, and with it, a huge change in politics.

John went back to his office and began preparing for Thursday's class on the Reagan Revolution. President Reagan was John's favorite president over the last 100 years. John was impressed that he was a vocal progressive for the first part of his life, saw the errors of his ways, and then change into an ultra-conservative Republican, almost Goldwaterist. He was impressed that Reagan communicated his plan to the American people in a way that was entirely logical. He was impressed by his ability to give people hope when hope probably was not there. He was impressed that Reagan surrounded himself with the smartest and brightest people in the world. However, John knew that Reagan had his faults—the biggest being that he was too trusting of the people around him. John also did not appreciate the massive increase in federal spending and increases to the debt during his term. He wanted to paint a balanced picture, but knew that would be terribly difficult.

Chapter 22

John awoke on Thursday morning excited about class that day. He enjoyed discussing the presidency of Ronald Reagan and the impact it had not only on the economy but the world stage. During Reagan's presidency, the United States became the sole superpower after Reagan's policies aided the implosion of the former Soviet Union. Reagan also helped America get back to a sense of hope and dominance in the world that was lost during the 1960s due to Vietnam and the economic problems of the 1970s. John again told himself to be impartial when discussing Reagan, but knew it was going to be tough. During breakfast, John discussed Reagan's presidency with Jenny. Jenny patiently listened, as she had the million times before. She could have probably written a book on Reagan based on conversations with her husband.

John walked into the lecture hall and displayed the following slide:

- Reagan took office when the country was still facing stagflation, another energy crisis in 1979, inflation in double-digits, unemployment well above 8%.
- Reagan heavily believed in the free-market – supply-side economics (Reaganomics) believed in lower taxes, lower regulations, and lower federal spending
- Reagan's first act was to eliminate price controls on domestic energy which was responsible for the 1979 energy crisis.
- Reagan cut federal tax rates by 25%, reduced regulations,
- Reagan also went head to head with unions – he fired all of the federal air traffic controllers
- In 1981, the economy went into a massive recession (actually worse than the one in 2007-2009). Unemployment was over 10%. The tax cuts shorten the recession cycle.
- After the recession, the economy grew, without inflation, the fastest in the last 40 years. Businesses added over 25 million jobs, and the government actually brought in more tax revenues than before.
- In 1983, Reagan "shored-up" social security by increasing the ages and reducing benefits.
- Negatives – federal spending actually increased during his term, deficits soared during his presidency.

He began by discussing the state of the economy in 1981 when Reagan took office. The economy was still under stagflation, which could have never happened under a true free market economy. John looked up and noticed that William Randolph had decided to join the discussion for the day. John smiled, and Randolph returned the gesture. John pointed out that Reagan was a supply-sider. Supply-side economics is built on the premise of providing companies with the ability to produce. The fruits of that production will work itself through the economy as a whole. Supply-side economics requires low taxes, fewer regulations and, in some cases, deregulation. These elements are believed to stimulate the economy. In other words, supply-side economics moves closer to a true free-market system. Critics called this economic policy either "voodoo" or "trickle-down" economics.

John explained that one of the first things that Reagan did was to eliminate the price controls that Nixon and Carter had initiated on energy, principally domestic oil. From that point forward, the country has not experienced another energy crisis. John pointed out that price controls caused the 1979 energy crisis.

Reagan also reduced federal tax rates by 25 percent, which were the biggest single decrease in the last seventy-five years. Reagan also went after the unions. In 1981, the air traffic controllers went on strike. Instead of ordering them back to work, Reagan simply fired them. John suggested that if the automotive companies had done the same thing back in the 1970s–2000s, it would not have been necessary for the federal government to bailout GM and Chrysler in 2009. John saw Randolph fidget a bit on that comment.

John continued by saying the United States' economy went into a massive recession in 1981. This recession was caused primarily by Federal Reserve Chairman Paul Volcker's change in monetary policy, which was to reduce the double-digit inflation. Unemployment rose above 10 percent, inflation was still above 10 percent, and GDP contracted 4.9 percent between 1980 and 1982. John asked how these numbers measured up with the 2007-2009 recession. Most of the students thought the most recent recession was much worse. John pointed out that inflation was under 2 percent, unemployment never exceeded 9.8 percent, and GDP contracted 4.3 percent. John told the class what politicians say is not necessarily the truth. For example, President Obama has continually said the 2007-2009 recession was the worst economic event since the Great Depression. This statement is simply not true. It is also pertinent to note that the Great Depression had numbers of inflation at double digits, unemployment at 25 percent, and 26.7 percent reduction in GDP. John pointed out that some of the biggest differences in the 1980–1982 and the 2007–2009 recessions are how robustly the economy grew afterwards. The aftermath of the 1980–1982 recession was growth of over 5 percent per year for the rest of the decade. So far, the aftermath of the 2007–2009 has been growth of around 2 percent and has currently fallen downward from that point. In other words, the policies that Reagan enacted allowed the economy to grow dramatically. Conversely, the policies enacted by Obama have stifled the economy's ability to grow. John promised more discussion on this subject later in the course.

He explained that from 1982 until 1989, businesses added twenty-five million people to the workforce as the economy grew. The most remarkable thing also happened: even with the lower tax rates, revenues to the federal government grew in total dollars and as a percentage of GDP. From 1985 and throughout the remainder of the decade, tax revenues remained above 32 percent and rose to 33 percent of GDP. He asked for explanations. He stated true wealth is created in the private sector and not in the government. He referred back to the multiplier effect discussed in a previous class. Reagan's tax cuts, deregulation, and reduction in regulations proved that the free market could produce more benefits than relying on the federal government. He noticed a frown had settled onto Randolph's face.

John showed the following slide:

Session 9 – The Reagan Revolution

Date	National Debt	Change	% Inc
9/30/1988	2,602,337,712,041	252,060,821,088	9.7%
9/30/1987	2,350,276,890,953	224,974,274,295	9.6%
9/30/1986	2,125,302,616,658	302,199,616,658	14.2%
9/30/1985	1,823,103,000,000	250,837,000,000	13.8%
9/30/1984	1,572,266,000,000	195,056,000,000	12.4%
9/30/1983	1,377,210,000,000	235,176,000,000	17.1%
9/30/1982	1,142,034,000,000	144,179,000,000	12.6%
9/30/1981	997,855,000,000	90,154,000,000	9.0%

- Even with more revenues, governmental spending increased every year
- Under Reagan's watch, the debt increased by $1.6 trillion (2011 expected amount).
- Reagan admitted that his greatest failure as President was the amount of debt he took on.

Source: www.usgovernmentspending.com

John, however, did point out one thing that Reagan did not do that he promised he would. Reagan did not reduce spending. As a matter of fact, spending remained about the same as a percentage of GDP during the entire decade. Spending stayed between 33 and 36 percent. Since revenues were between 31 and 33 percent each year, the country had deficits, and the deficits were large, ranging from $100 billion at the beginning of the decade to $300 billion at the end of the decade. Reagan stated his biggest failure as president was the amount of the debt he charged to the country's credit card. All told, Reagan increased the debt by $1.6 trillion, which is similar to what Obama is running up every year now. John asked if there were any questions. He answered a few of the questions and adjourned the session. Randolph left immediately after class.

Chapter 23

At the conclusion of class on Thursday, John could enjoy spring break, which was early this year— in March instead of April. John had promised Jenny, their children and grandchildren that they could go to Aspen for a weeklong ski vacation and enjoy the last hurrah to winter. He had never been a skier, and Jenny had long given up on the pastime. They loved time together sipping coffee at the lodge while the gang skied. In accordance with his retirement agreement with Smith Goldman, John was able to use the company jet for a specified amount of time each year for the next five years. John and the gang headed for the Newport News Airport, boarded the Gulfstream V, and took off for Aspen. Two and one-half hours later, the jet came to a stop at the Aspen Airport. From the airport, it was about a twenty-five minute drive to the cottage. The grandchildren were already asking when they could go skiing.

After dinner that night, John took the grandchildren over to an ice skating rink for a couple of hours. By ten p.m., everyone was ready for bed. The next morning, John, Jenny, the children and grandchildren were at the ski lodge at nine thirty for a day of skiing. John and Jenny stayed in the warm lodge by the crackling fire while everyone else braved the cold.

By Sunday, John was already bored and started to think about class the following week. His mind always raced and never allowed him a real vacation. The subject matter for the next class was the housing bubble. John knew that most of the students probably had incorrect facts of why the housing bubble started. He also knew that the housing market was still suffering as housing prices continued to fall. Many people in the United States were still losing their homes to foreclosure due to the lack of making timely mortgage payments. The correction to the housing bubble was not easy and would not be quick. The discussion for next Tuesday would be very stimulating.

As the week wore on, John continued to reflect on the prior sessions and how the students were being introduced to other ways to look at history. He was surprised how little push-back he received from the students since the material was wholly contrary to what they had been taught since elementary school. He was also surprised that Randolph continued to visit the classroom. Since the earlier sessions related to history, John was curious if Randolph would become more vocal during discussions of current events. Since John's previous firm had bought and sold mortgage-backed securities, would Randolph confront him about being part of the reason for the housing bubble? John was ready for the class to start.

As the family packed suitcases and loaded the airplane for the return trip to Williamsburg, John smiled as he saw refreshed but tired faces. Everyone appeared to have had a fabulous time on the vacation. As the plane left the hanger and taxied toward the runway, John remembered the frequent trips that he took when he was in private industry and how very infrequently he had the opportunity to come to Aspen for an entire week while Jenny and the children were young. This observation made John remorseful that his profession had stolen his family time. The pace of life now was conducive to quality family time, and he hoped this trip was a forerunner to memorable times ahead.

Chapter 24

John walked into the classroom about ten minutes before the starting time. He noticed William Randolph perched in his usual seat and walked over. They shook hands and kindly greeted each other. John told Randolph that today's discussion was on the housing bubble. John urged Randolph to speak up if he wanted to add to the discussion. Randolph was shocked. He had been given the freedom to address any potential inaccuracies that John may bring forth during the session. Randolph doubted that he would take advantage of such an opportunity out of respect for John's authority in the class.

John told the class that today's discussion was on the housing bubble. The following slide was shown:

Session 10 – The Housing Bubble - Concepts

- **Housing bubble** happens when valuations in real property rapidly increase until they reach unsustainable levels and eventually the bubble "burst" causes a many year freefall in real estate prices.
- In the US, house prices started increasing in the 1980s and continued to increase until 2006. In 2006, house prices started to fall.
- In the 1990s, **sub prime loans** became available. Sub prime loans (near-prime, non-prime, second-chance loans) means loans to people who have difficulty maintaining the repayment schedule.
- Proponents of subprime lending argued that the practice extended credit to people who would otherwise not have access to the credit market.
- Often subprime loans would be ARMs (adjustable rate mortgages).
- **Mortgage backed securities** – a type of investment by which the originator entity would package good mortgages (FHA etc) and group them with sub prime loans. These securities would be sold to an entity upstream including Freddie Mac and Fannie Mae.
- **Community Reinvestment Act of 1977** – the law requiring commercial banks and saving associations to lend to all borrowers including low and moderate income people (Substantially changed in 1992-1999).
- **Discount rate** – the rate in which banks can borrow money from the Federal Reserve. It is set by the Chairman of the Federal Reserve.

He explained that a housing bubble occurs when demand significantly outpaces supply. When there is a vast imbalance, the price valuations become unsustainable, and the bubble bursts. John explained that is what happened in 2006.

He explained the concepts of subprime loans, and how irresponsible it was for mortgage companies to allow these loans. Most subprime loans were adjustable rate mortgages with rates that could change every year. He explained mortgage-backed securities whereby originators of subprime loans could reduce their risk by bundling bad mortgages with good mortgages. The federal government allowed these securities to be created and traded. John discussed the Community Reinvestment Act of 1977 and how this law was unconstitutional because it required banks to lend to people who showed a low likelihood of repaying the loan. He also explained the substantial modifications made in the 1990s to this law. Finally, John discussed how the Federal Reserve used the discount rate to keep inflation in check.

John showed the next slide:

- Item 1 – 1977 - President Carter signs the **Community Reinvestment Act** into law – Groundbreaking event.
- Item 2 – Early 1990s – President Clinton "**doubled-down**" on the Community Reinvestment Act. Requires more lending to low income borrowers.
- Item 3 – Early 1990s - **Sub Prime Lending** created. This allowed banks to lend to people with little or no money down for real estate.
- Item 4 – 1990s – **Dot Com Event** – The increase in Dot Com Stock valuations created a lot of people with money. This "extra" money allowed housing prices to start to increase dramatically.
- Item 5 – 1990s – **Mortgage Backed Securities** – The federal regulators allowed for the bundling of mortgages to be sold within financial markets.
- Item 6 – 1990s – **Baby Boomers**' kids leave the nest. Boomers are behind on retirement nest eggs, start upgrading real estate because it is their biggest asset
- Item 7 – 1990s – **Federal Reserve**, specifically Alan Greenspan, starts to focus on inflation using discount rate to drive economy. Late 1990s, Dot Com busted.
- Item 8 – Early 2000s – US enters into 2 recessions (one caused by Dot Com Bust and other due to 2 wars). Greenspan keeps the **discount rate very low** – allows for massive borrowing by consumers.
- Item 9 – **Housing Market on Fire** – Housing starts in 2005 were 1.2 million – in 1990s, 600,000 per year, excess supply of housing

John continued by saying that the unconstitutional Community Reinvestment Act of 1977 started the chain of events that caused the housing bubble. When President Clinton "doubled-down" on the requirements that banks must lend to people who are not likely to repay, it created a scenario in which anyone could borrow money. It did not matter whether the money could be paid back or not. Banks found a way to meet the new requirements by creating subprime loans. These loans carried higher interest rates and typically were adjustable-rate mortgages. This allowed the mortgage rates to change annually. These loans also allowed for lower upfront money and in some cases no money down. This practice of writing loans was terribly irresponsible of the banks, but it was allowed by the federal government. During the 1990s, dot-com companies were springing up everywhere, but they generated little cash. Whenever something seems to be too good to be true, it usually is. The dot-com bubble burst in 1999. However in the 1990s, a lot of wealth was transferred as people invested in these ventures. With newfound money, young people and fortunate investors were bidding up housing prices in California, Nevada, and other areas of the country. By that time, banks were starting to worry about the subprime loans on their balance sheets. They asked for the creation of mortgage-backed securities that could be bought and sold among financial institutions. These instruments consisted of good mortgages and bad mortgages. The underlying thought was that the good mortgages would prop up the bad ones. What the banks did not expect were high foreclosure rates.

In 1999 President Clinton repealed the Glass Steagall Act, allowing investment banks such as Goldman Sachs and Lehman Brothers to start lending money to consumers for things like mortgages. Previously, investment banks could only issue investment securities, and commercial banks, such as Bank of America and Citibank, could lend money to consumers. Even though Clinton allowed investment banks to lend money, the government did not require the investment banks to have minimum leverage ratios. This would be a serious problem later on as the value of the underlying collateral fell.

In addition, the 1990s brought the first realization by baby boomers that their retirement nest eggs were too bare. Some baby boomers started trading up their homes in hopes of a big appreciation in value. This also caused an artificial increase in real estate valuations. To prevent high inflation and to keep the United States out of a recession, the Federal Reserve kept the discount rate too low for too long. This allowed banks to lend money cheaply. It also allowed the Americans to keep borrowing at historically low interest rates. Finally, the housing market was on fire as new building starts were too high to maintain. From 2000 to 2003, new housing starts were abnormally high. John concluded that all of these factors caused the housing bubble and led to unsustainable housing prices and a glut of houses available for purchase.

John asked for discussion as to which group has the most culpability. The students had a host of answers, and John knew that Randolph had answers too. John showed the following slide:

Session 10 – The Housing Bubble – Who is to Blame?

- Lot of blame to go around – biggest culprit was the federal government
  1. Community Reinvestment Act – required banks to lend
  2. Federal Regulators requiring more lending to unqualified people
  3. Allowing the selling of Mortgage Backed Securities
  4. Allowing the discount rate to be held so low for so long
  5. Bailouts (to be discussed later in the course)
- American people
  1. Starting in 1990, the American people took on a massive amount of new debt
  2. Took on debt that they knew they couldn't afford
  3. People were willing and were allowed to simply walk away from the asset and loan (foreclosures)
- Banks – should have never allowed sub-prime loans, petitioned for mortgage backed securities, asked for bailout money (to be discussed later)

John stated that the federal government was the main culprit of the housing bubble. He noticed Randolph staring a hole through him now. He discussed each of the events in which the federal government had a direct hand then directed the conversation to the responsibility of the American people. If everyone was responsible for their own actions, the reduction in housing prices would have been a blip on the economy. People would have had to put money down on houses, therefore they would have equity even after a valuation correction. If bankruptcy and foreclosure laws were not so utterly lax, fewer people would have taken advantage of these laws to fix their mistakes. In a nutshell, the American people were allowed to act irresponsibly, and the nanny state was there to bail them out. Randolph was fidgeting now. Finally, John stated that banks were also responsible because of the creation of subprime loans and petitioning for mortgage-backed securities. He concluded by saying that the overall debacle would not have happened if the federal government stayed within the enumerated powers of the Constitution, and the American people would have acted more responsibly. Randolph's face was bright red now.

John asked the students how the housing market would be corrected. Most students believed the government needed to get out the way, but few had specific solutions.

Session 10 – The Housing Bubble – How to Fix It?

- How not to fix it – bank bailouts (government selecting winners and losers and calling it "too big to fail"), forcing mergers (Bank of America and Merrill Lynch), bailing out homeowners who are upside down, implementing new banking regulations
- At the end of the day, there were simply too many houses that were overpriced and too few buyers.
- As April 2011, the market is still decreasing because the bottom hasn't been found. The government needs to let the market find its bottom.
- Government needs to get out of the housing market for good – eliminate Freddie and Fannie immediately.
- Repeal the Community Reinvestment Act – government should not dictate who banks lend money to.
- Bring formal charges against Paulson and Bernanke for the undue pressure put on banks to either buy troubled banks or forcing banks to accept funds they didn't want. Both are guilty of misuse of their respective offices.
- Real extreme – systematically eliminate the Federal Reserve

John started the discussion on how not to fix the housing market. Bank bailouts, forced mergers, homeowner bailouts, and implemented new banking regulations did not fix the housing market. In some cases, it probably prolonged the downturn. John explained what happened could have been learned in economics 101. There were simply too many high-priced houses available for people who wanted them. As of April 2011 the bottom of the housing market still had not been met, and it could take a couple more years. John mentioned that the federal government needed to get out the housing market and privatize Freddie Mac and Fannie Mae. He also suggested the elimination of the Community Reinvestment Act. Formal criminal charges should be brought against Hank Paulson and Ben Bernanke for the misuse of their respective offices. Finally, John stated it would probably make a significant deal of sense for the government to formulate a plan to eliminate the Federal Reserve. Randolph was breathing fire now.

John answered some questions by the students and dismissed the class. He was collecting his papers when Randolph approached the front desk and asked why John did not think more of the blame should not be placed on the banks and Wall Street. John felt that the regulations created by the federal government were the main factor. If there were no regulations by the federal government, the housing bubble would have never happened because banks would not have gotten upside down on the loans. Besides, Wall Street did not repeal the Glass Steagall Act allowing investment banks to lend money to consumers.

"Bull," Randolph said in a loud voice as he walked off mumbling.

John snickered because he enjoyed getting under the skins of liberals on such issues.

Chapter 25

On Wednesday, John had lunch with Thornton Smith at the President's House. He knew there would be the standard request for a donation for this project or that project. He also anticipated some discussion on how the class was going. John was sure that some of the liberal establishment, who called themselves professors, had voiced their displeasure of the subject matter and the positions he had taken.

John walked around the left side of the J. Christopher Wren building and up to the door of the President's House. He knocked on the door, and Smith warmly greeted him with the familiar toothy smile and invited him into the house. After a few moments of pleasantries, John followed Smith into the dining room for lunch. During lunch, Smith "put the bite" on John and asked for a donation to refurbish the Crim Dell, a semi-circle bridge over a small body of water at the base of the Sunken Gardens. It was a college superstition that if a young man met a young woman on the bridge and they kissed, they would get married. Most William and Mary co-eds envisioned themselves on the bridge with their Prince Charming. John promised that he would discuss the donation with Jenny that night but did not think it would be a problem. After all, this romantic landmark would need to continue to be a precursor to happy marriages!

After lunch, the men retired to Smith's office, just across the hall from the dining room. Smith asked John how the class was progressing. John stated he had been surprised at how the students were receiving the material and looking at the events of history from a point of view other than liberal. The students seemed to enjoy the class, and he enjoyed reading the responses to the midterm exams. John turned the tables on Smith and asked what he had heard about the course and how it was going. Smith reflected he had heard both positive and negative reports, which John found to be typical with Smith, who was known to be a true politician about things like this—never taking one side or the other and also never revealing the sources. John pressed him further but did not get terribly far. After about an hour, John thanked Smith for lunch and departed the house. As always, it was a pleasure to partake of a meal at the famous historical building with Thornton Smith.

Chapter 26

On Thursday morning, John arrived at the college around eight thirty and went to his office to answer e-mails. He received one from Randolph requesting a conference that afternoon. John responded back in the affirmative and hurried to class. When he arrived there, he noticed that Randolph was absent.

He presented the following slide and began by saying that today's discussion was on the United States' Budget and the impacts of entitlements:

Session 11 – United State Budget and Entitlements
In millions

	Revenues	Spending	Deficit	Debt
Beginning				5,911
Clinton 2000	2,026	1,789	236	5,674
Bush 2001	1,991	2,125	(134)	5,808
Bush 2002	1,853	2,273	(420)	6,228
Bush 2003	1,783	2,338	(555)	6,783
Bush 2004	1,880	2,476	(596)	7,379
Bush 2005	2,154	2,708	(554)	7,933
Bush 2006	2,407	2,981	(574)	8,507
Bush 2007	2,568	3,069	(501)	9,008
Bush 2008	2,524	3,502	(978)	9,986
Obama 2009	2,108	3,520	(1,412)	11,398
Obama 2010	2,163	3,456	(1,293)	12,691
Obama 2011	2,174	3,819	(1,645)	14,336

Source: www.usgovernmentspending.com

John directed the students to the fact that revenues have increased by 17.5 percent over the decade, but spending had increased by 155 percent. He further pointed out that the entitlement programs—Social Security (pensions), Medicare and Medicaid (health care), and welfare increased by $1 trillion during the decade. Military spending has increased by $513 billion. He also pointed out that entitlement spending plus interest is almost equal to what the United States brings in from taxes.

John asked the class for discussion on the options that America has to reduce the deficit. John explained one could cut spending; one could increase taxes; or one could do a combination of both. Republicans typically believe the way to fix the budget is to cut spending. Democrats believe that one must tax people more. The real solution is a combination of both. That is the easy solution to the problem, but the hardest part of the problem is the balancing of spending cuts to tax increases.

John decided that he would share his solution with the class. He believed that a new consumption tax would be the only tax that would not have a negative impact to the economy. On spending cuts, the solution would require some changes to formulas and benefits (entitlement programs) and some would require true cost cutting, such as a reduction in the federal government. John told the class that in his mind, a 3-to-1 ratio was the best ratio. For every three dollars of spending cuts, one could increase taxes by a dollar. For example, if the federal government wanted to levy a value-added tax of 3 percent, that would raise approximately $420 billion of additional revenues. At the same time, the government would need to cut spending by $1.26 billion. This would eliminate the 2010 deficit and payback approximately $100 billion on the debt. John asked the students where spending should be cut. Collectively, they believed a large percentage should come from the entitlement programs and defense since they are the biggest cost items. John shared his formula with the class.

Session 11 – Spending Cuts

Spending Cuts
Mandatory Spending

Pensions	100.0
Healthcare	100.0
Welfare	305.7
Interest	
Total Mandatory Spending	505.7

Discretionary Spending

Education	47.6
Defense	220.0
Protection	8.6
Transportation	29.3
General Govt	4.8
Jobs Creation	385.0
Other Spending	48.1
Balance	10.9
Total Discretionary Spending	754.3
Total Spending	1,260.0

He explained that both discretionary and mandatory spending has to be reduced. The largest item to cut would be President Obama's job-creation program. The free market will create jobs, not the federal government. Unemployment insurance would be eliminated. People can find work if there is not a crutch around holding them up. Defense would have to take a considerable reduction. All other discretionary spending would be reduced back to 2008 levels. The formulas for Social Security and health care would have to be changed to save $200 billion. John asked the class their thoughts about his proposal. The students believed more should come out of Social Security and health care. John told the class that this was his idea. Everyone would look at this a different way. Democrats have politicized Paul Ryan's plan, which would reduce health-care costs instead of coming up with a plan on their own. That is the problem with the budget—no one wants to be the adult at the head of the table. The president should be leading this deficit reduction effort, as opposed to trying to get elected. The deficit is out of control.

John said they would discuss out-of-control spending and its impact on the economy at a later session. He asked each of the students to propose a way to eliminate the deficit and begin reducing the debt of more than $14 trillion. John stated they would review their ideas at the next class and asked that each solution come in a PowerPoint slide on a memory stick.

Later that day William Randolph knocked on John's office door. They shook hands, and John offered Randolph a chair. Randolph asked if John was serious about offering his opinion during class. John told Randolph that he welcomed his opinions, and it would give the students potentially two differing points of view. Randolph seemed a bit taken back by this statement, and he reinitiated his statement with John agreeing. John told Randolph that at the next class, the students were to provide their opinions on how to balance the United States budget and start reducing the debt. Randolph asked John to share his opinion. John shared the materials and discussion for the course that day. They debated ways to reduce the deficit without hurting the economy or creating more poverty in America. When they looked up, it was after five p.m. John invited Randolph over to The Willows for dinner so that they could continue their discussion. Randolph graciously accepted. John called Jenny from the truck to alert her about the last minute dinner guest. She suggested that he grill some steaks, and he willingly agreed.

Chapter 27

John arrived at the college on Tuesday at eight a.m. and read some e-mail. He looked forward to the students' ideas on how to repair the deficit. He left for class about fifteen minutes before starting time.

The students were highly anxious to share their ideas. Some were utterly foolish—multidigit tax rate increases to the elimination of Social Security. There were some proposals that displayed creativity. The first one was from John Wilson:

John Wilson's Proposal on Eliminating the Deficit

Revenues:	
Revenues from Countries Relying on our Military	300
4% VAT Tax	600
Additional Revenues	900
Spending Cuts:	
Defense	305
Jobs Creation	385
Education	53
Transportation	42
General Govt	2
Other Spending	72
Total Spending Cuts	859
Total New Revenues and Spending Cuts	1,759
Reduction in Debt	500
Year to Eliminate the Debt	28

Entitlements would have to set not to increase past current levels.

Wilson stated that his goal was to try to pay off the debt of around $14 trillion within thirty years. The first requirement would be the elimination of the deficit. New revenues would come from a 4 percent value-added tax and requiring countries that use the US military for their protection to pay for it. John was genuinely impressed with this idea. Wilson said spending would have to be reduced back to 2004 levels. Finally, Wilson suggested America move troops out of Iraq and Afghanistan immediately. He stated that the United States would need to run surpluses of $500 billion per year in order to pay the debt back in less than thirty years. John asked about ObamaCare. Wilson stated that would have to be repealed. John was impressed with this proposal.

A second proposal was from Susan Billows:

```
                    Susan Billows' Proposal
  Taxes:
  Reduce Corp Tax Rate to 20%                          (95)
  Expected increase in GDP (10%)                        290
  Flat Tax (Eliminate all Deductions)                   220

  Total New Taxes                                        415

  Spending:
  Move Education to States                             (150)
  40% Reduction in Defense                             (349)
  Eliminate Jobs Creation                              (385)
  Revised Unemployment Ins.                            (125)
  Means Test SS/Medicare                               (325)
  Reduce all other spending to 2008                    (102)
  Limit time on Medicaid                               (125)

  Total Spending Cuts                                (1,561)

  Grand Total                                        (1,976)

              Surpluses to be used to reduce debt
```

John asked Billows about the flat tax. She stated that the rate would be 20 percent across the board. John also asked about means testing on Social Security and Medicare. Billows stated that it is not fair, but it is a necessity. She also added that Social Security and

Medicare would be phased out, and the surpluses would increase over time. Billows also suggested time limits on welfare and Medicaid, which would stop the generational use of the programs. John was tremendously impressed.

John reiterated that the purpose of this session was to get the students thinking about how to fix the problem. Secondarily, it shows there are no right answers. The real question is when to get started. He mentioned that a lot of people think the answer is either all tax increases or all spending cuts. It will take both to get this problem fixed. They discussed a few of the other students' proposals, and he collected all of the memory sticks. He thanked the students for their contributions and said the next class would involve a discussion on the zero-liability voter.

John walked back to his office and started to review some e-mails. He received an e-mail from Hank Johnson, the chairman of the Virginia Republican Party. It asked if they could get together for dinner one day next week. John had known Hank since their college days. John wrote a quick e-mail back and invited him to The Willows for dinner next week. He copied Jenny on the note so she would not be caught off guard. John wondered what Hank wanted; they had not spoken in about six months.

Chapter 28

On Thursday morning, John parked his Ford F-150 in the facility parking lot near Dominion Hall and walked to his office. Williamsburg in the spring is the most beautiful place on earth. John found himself whistling as he walked along the bricked sidewalks to the business school building. He thought back to when he was an undergrad going to class. Suddenly he felt terribly old as he looked at the "babies" he saw on the sidewalks. He walked past Old Dominion Hall, where he and his brother lived their senior year (due to a very good lottery number given to him). He wondered if Dominos' Pizza still had the policy of "thirty minutes or it is free." He truly loved the "College of Knowledge" as William and Mary students called it.

He went to his office and read some e-mails. It was phenomenal he received so many e-mails even though he was a new professor. At nine twenty a.m., he walked down to class. As he walked in, he noticed Randolph in his familiar seat on the back row near one of the exits. He smiled and waved at him, and the gesture was returned with the same gusto. John knew that today might get a vocal rise out of Randolph because there was a lot of passion on the side of wealth inequality in the country, in particular in the college scene.

John presented the following slide:

- NY Times reported that 47% of Americans pay no federal income taxes (2009)
- In 2007, the number was 38%
- 18,000 people making over $500k pay zero income taxes
- GE, one of the largest and most profitable companies in the world, paid no income taxes.
- The article goes to say a bunch of mess about tax credits etc, but at the end of day it is true.
- How did we get to this situation?
- Some would say the rich have gotten richer at the expense of the poor.
- Free market dictates winner and losers – the problem is there is another factor – the government interference has made it possible for it to change the true winners and losers
- Who should have been the winners/losers with GM in 2009 – No winners – everyone should have lost (unions, bond holders stockholders etc). Instead the winners were the unions and losers were the American people, bond holders, stockholders.

My opinion – the entitlement state (welfare, social security, medicare, medicaid) and bailouts have made the American people completely reliant on "Big Brother." Generation after generation has put their complete trust in the government for "checks" and bailouts when they make bad decisions.

John asked the student to discuss how America got to the place in which 47 percent of Americans pay zero federal income taxes. The students had a host of answers, but John was not satisfied with any of them. John asked Randolph what he thought. Randolph was obviously not ready for a direct question, but he stated that wealth distribution in America has eroded over the years resulting in only the rich having a chance to succeed. John asked for explanations on how that happened. Randolph continued by saying the free-market system, while it has a lot of benefits, has some considerable problems. Greed allows people to restrict free trade and create unfair markets, with Enron and the California energy crisis as an example. John wanted to know who created the regulations in California that kept other companies from coming in and trying to gain a footprint in the markets. Randolph pointed out regulations in energy have been proven to be the most advantageous to the customer. John knew that was the most common argument, but there were many holes in it. He knew that true competition was the only way in which the consumers would see the lowest possible prices. He decided to move to the next question.

John asked the students if they thought the entitlement state America has endured over the last seventy years has had an impact on "wealth distribution." Most students sat intensely silently awaiting a response from Randolph. After a few uncomfortable moments, Randolph responded that while the entitlement programs of FDR and LBJ "probably" had an impact, it was likely insignificant and not the real reason the "rich get richer and the poor get poorer." John asked Randolph to expand on his views. He continued that greed and unfair business practices probably had more to do with the inequality than anything else. John rebutted this statement as false. The federal government created affirmative action and quotas, and the balance has still become more unbalanced. The creation of complete reliance on the federal and state governments, which has been passed down as a "birthright," has created a permanent "underclass" which requires more and more assistance from "Big Brother." Welfare, unemployment payments, Medicaid, food stamps, and so forth have continued to increase even when the economy is robustly growing. John looked directly at Randolph, and most of the students anticipated a response. Randolph refuted by stating that opportunities were not equal among the culprits. Most people collecting welfare are people with one-parent families; therefore, the chances of those people succeeding would be significantly decreased.

"Bull," John stated. Motivation comes from within, not from the government or external sources. As children watch their parent or parents receiving benefits from the government, they believe they are entitled to the same benefits. Instead of wanting to be "better" than their parents, they will simply fall back to the same results.

John asked if Americans who do not pay any federal income taxes be allowed to vote. Most students believed they should be able to vote. Randolph stated that paying taxes should not have anything to do with voting. The US Constitution was abundantly clear in this regard. John asked if it was fair for people having "no skin in the game" deciding the leadership of the country. Remember, the Revolution War was fought over "taxation without representation." This was the inverse of the argument "representation without taxation." John proposed that these people were "zero-liability voters." As long as their "checks" continued, they would vote for the person who was best for them and their continued enrichment. Most students changed their original thought and thought there should be a tax litmus test. Randolph fumed and stated that was unconstitutional. John suggested a constitutional amendment to ensure that only tax-paying Americans be allowed to vote. Why not let illegal aliens vote? What is the real difference?

Randolph was getting red in the face as his disagreement continued to build. He felt that this was not the intent of the founding fathers. When the "playing field" was not balanced, the inequality would continue. John decided that this was an impasse and asked the class to voice their opinions. Surprisingly, the class saw both sides of the discussion. This pleased John. The students asked questions of both Randolph and John and seemed intrigued by the discussion. John had to end the class at eleven o'clock to make sure the students got to their next classes on time. Randolph walked down the steps to the front of the class, shook John's hand, offered a smile, and left the class. John thought that was the best class of the semester. Several students came up to say they truly enjoyed the class that day. John decided to give Randolph a call before the next class to ensure that he would attend for continued debate and discussion. It reminded John about his reading of the Lincoln-Douglas debates of 1858. John looked forward to the next class.

Chapter 29

John and Jenny had a fabulous weekend with the grandchildren as they spent time fishing at the pond and riding horses on the former plantation. The grandchildren reminded John of the subject matter for the next class—education, specifically how much money had been spent over the last fifty years and how little there had been to show for it. The United States spends more money per student than any country in the world and ranks near the bottom in performance rankings. Teacher unions have become extremely strong as to enable "incompetent teachers" to stay in the system and have driven the cost up so that most states are running deficits. He wanted the students to understand that "throwing money" at problems makes them worse. John called Randolph, and talked to him for over an hour. They discussed the previous class and how well it went. Both men looked forward to Tuesday's class.

On Tuesday morning, John walked into his office and read his e-mail. There were many e-mails that were complementary of the last class from his students. Most of them wanted to know if the class structure would continue in the same manner. John hoped so.

He walked down to the lecture hall and began class with the following slide:

Session 13 – Department of Education

- In 2010, America ranked 12th out of top 12 industrialized countries

	Total Spent (In Billions)	Annual Spending/ Child	Math Scores	Science Scores	Points per $ Spend	Rank
United States	$ 809.6	$ 7,743	474	489	0.12	12
Japan	$ 160.5	$ 3,756	523	531	0.28	5
Germany	$ 129.8	$ 4,682	504	516	0.22	6
United Kingdom	$ 122.6	$ 5,834	495	515	0.17	11
France	$ 121.0	$ 5,541	496	495	0.18	10
Brazil	$ 114.0	$ 1,683	370	390	0.45	2
Russia	$ 86.9	$ 1,850	476	479	0.52	1
Mexico	$ 74.9	$ 1,975	406	410	0.41	3
Canada	$ 65.4	$ 5,749	527	534	0.18	8
South Korea	$ 61.6	$ 3,759	547	522	0.28	4
Australia	$ 41.8	$ 5,766	520	527	0.18	9
Finland	$ 10.0	$ 5,653	548	563	0.20	7

Source: The Heritage Foundation

The class discussion began with how much money America spent in 2010 on education: $810 billion. The next closest to the United States was Japan at $161 billion. John pointed out that the United States spends 25 percent more per child than the next highest country, the United Kingdom. What is totally unbelievable is the two top spenders per student are ranked eleventh and twelfth out of twelve countries. In the 1950s, the United States was the number one country in the world based on test scores. John asked his students what the conclusion was to all of this. Most students agreed that the United States had failed children and dramatically needed to change the current system.

John asked what would happen if the Department of Education was disbanded and their functions transferred back to the states. He asked Randolph for his thoughts. Randolph stated he agreed sweeping changes were needed in the Department of Education, and a lot of the functions needed to be moved to the states, but he felt that a complete elimination of the department would be too drastic. The department provides standards that the entire country uses. John stated that each state needs to determine standards based on what the population and future businesses would need. John stated that the "true" purpose of an education should be to enable the student to have necessary skills in order to find worthy employment. Randolph emphatically disagreed. He stated that education should be a means for students to be exposed to different and engaging subject matter to increase their intellect. Money and a career should come in due course. John asked each student in class to think about why they are in college. All but two students said they were there to build skills necessary to secure future employment. The administrators of colleges liked to believe that the purpose of college was enlightenment, but students and parents want colleges to prepare their children for careers. Randolph was frowning and sternly stated that not all college administrators thought that way. He continued that college administrators and professors were not people in ivory towers removed from the "real world." In response, John agreed not all college administrators and professors were removed from the real world, however tenure for college professors existed. Nowhere in the business world would one find tenure. Randolph retorted that tenure was necessary for colleges to keep the best and most talented so that business would not steal them. Colleges do not pay the same as private industry. John decided to let those comments slide.

John steered the discussion back to the original question. Should the federal government disband the Department of Education? All but two students agreed that the department should be eliminated. Randolph vehemently shook his head negatively.

As it was getting close to the end of the class, John mentioned that Randolph was a former member of the Virginia House of Delegates and has had to deal with a lot of the questions the class has been contemplating. He also mentioned that Randolph had spent many hours on television answering questions, particularly around presidential elections. Finally, John pointed out Randolph would join class in the future as his schedule permitted.

Most of the class looked at Randolph with respect. Randolph thanked John for the introduction and looked forward to future classes and balanced debates. John laughed, nodded to Randolph and dismissed the class. John then invited Randolph to join him at a seat in front of the class, but Randolph decided to stay in the back for the time being. They laughed, shook hands, and walked out together. The debate continued over lunch at Paul's Deli. John noticed a couple of students in the booth directly across from them listening intently on the conversation. This amused John tremendously.

Chapter 30

On Wednesday night, Hank Johnson, the chairman of the Virginia Republican Party, came to dinner at The Willows. John was very curious about his initiating this dinner meeting. At first he thought Hank needed a sizable donation to steer Virginia away from Obama in 2012. After all, it had been since 1964 when Virginia last voted for a Democrat in a presidential election. John thought it could be an extremely intriguing dinner.

Hank arrived at The Willows about six thirty p.m. John always liked to grill when guests visited, in particularly during the spring. Jenny laid out three filets on the counter, because everyone knows that steaks are better if they are prepared at room temperature. John started the charcoal chimney, and the briquettes were almost ready. John poured Hank a drink and led him out to the patio for conversation around the grill. John poured the ready charcoal into the pit and put the steaks on the grill. The steaks would take about ten minutes. Dinner was served around seven o'clock in the terrace off the patio.

After dinner, Hank and John adjourned to John's office. Hank asked John how his class was going at the college. John revealed that he was truly enjoying bringing a conservative point of view to the liberal arts college. Hank quickly got to the point of his seeking this meeting. He said that a lot of people in the party wanted John to consider running for office. The state Republicans wanted him to run for the US Senate in the seat that would be vacated by Democrat Jim Webb. It was time for the progressive agenda to end. John looked at Hank quite dumbfounded and told him that he was utterly ridiculous. Hank insisted he would win if he ran for office. They discussed the subject for almost two hours. At the end of the conversation, John told Hank he would give it some consideration.

As John and Jenny were getting ready for bed, Jenny asked what Hank wanted. John bluntly stated that Hank wanted him to run for the US Senate in the seat being vacated by Jim Webb. Jenny laughed and asked him what he thought. They cut off the lights but lay awake for hours discussing the possibility of a campaign, the pros and cons of the election process, and a potential Senate seat.

Chapter 31

John woke up the next morning thinking about the conversation that he had with Hank Johnson the night before. John had once thought about running for office, but put that notion behind him when he realized that elections were a popularity contest more than about fixing things wrong with America. It did not matter what the candidate said; it was much more important how the candidate looked and spoke. John's idealist bubble of public office was burst about twenty years ago by the realization that only the pretty and the well-spoken could get voted into office. He was not sure if he wanted to go through the process of having the press research every time he had a bowel movement during his life. He thought it was rather interesting he was offered this opportunity when his next session was on the causes of the financial meltdown. A lot of people were blaming investment banking firms, one of which he used to head.

John arrived at the college about eight a.m., walked into his office, read his e-mail, and answered the majority of them. At around nine fifteen, he walked down to the lecture hall. As he entered, he noticed that William Randolph was in his usual seat. They exchanged mutual smiles.

John put the following slide on the projector:

- 1938 – FDR created Fannie Mae – takes mortgage loans off of mortgage lenders so they could make more loans. These mortgages are guaranteed by the federal government.
- 1968 – Fannie Mae spins off Ginnie Mae which guarantees off mortgage loans. Ginnie Mae becomes a governmental sponsored entity (GSE).
- 1970 – Congress creates Freddie Mac (a GSE) to purchase mortgages from S&L. Since the federal government is guaranteeing these loans, it doesn't show the true debt that the federal government is taking on.
- Late 1970s, mortgages are pooled and the pools are sliced into tranches – sets the foundation for mortgage backed securities.
- November 2000 – Department of Housing and Urban Development requires Fannie Mae to dedicate 50% of its business to low and moderate income families.
- October 2004 – SEC suspends net capital rule for five firms – Goldman, Merrill Lynch, Lehman Bros, Bear Sterns and Morgan Stanley. They are able to lever up 20, 30 or even 40 to 1 – buy massive amounts of mortgage-backed securities.
- Fall of 2005 – Booming housing market halts abruptly – prices drop by 3.3%
- Beginning of 2006 – mortgage failure rates start to increase.
- September 2008 – Fed takes over Fannie and Freddie – owned or guaranteed $6 trillion

John stated that the subject matter for today was the financial meltdown of 2008–2010. Most economists believed that the meltdown ended in 2010; however, John believed that there were still pockets of insufficient liquidity. In 2008, there simply was not enough short-term credit available in the market. The financial meltdown was created by the events surrounding the housing market bust, but there were a lot of other factors and errors. Randolph was sitting on the edge of his seat. John discussed that Fannie Mae was created in 1938 as part of FDR's New Deal. This program purchased loans from mortgage lenders (commercial banks) and returned the cash to the banks so they could lend again. The money used to purchase these loans was an obligation of the federal government, since they guaranteed Fannie Mae. FDR had overstepped his Constitutional authority by allowing this to happen. John asked Randolph to voice his thoughts. Randolph stated that back in 1938 when the economy was going through a decade long depression, it was a suitable solution. However, he agreed that the benefit it caused did not justify the problems it would cause later. John stated the real unfortunate problem is the government's debt had been grossly understated for years. The guarantee did not show up as a potential liability.

John continued that during the Clinton Administration, the Department of Housing and Urban Development required Fannie Mae to lend 50 percent of its loans to low- and moderate-income families. As interest rates were low, more speculation and vacation homes were being purchased, thus requiring more and more unqualified loans to be made. Randolph said real estate speculation caused a lot more problems than loans made to low- and moderate-income families. John retorted saying in 2006, only 28 percent of the loans under Fannie Mae and Freddie Mac were for speculation and vacation homes. The remaining 72 percent were for primary residences, in which over 50 percent were required to be made to low- and moderate-income families. Therefore, by strict math and probability, the majority of the bogus loans were made to low- and moderate-income families.

John stated that the final nail in the coffin was when the SEC suspended the net capital rule for five investment firms—Goldman Sachs, Merrill Lynch, Lehman Brothers, Bear Sterns, and Morgan Stanley. John put the following slide on the projector:

- Financialization – financial system expansion and becoming more fragile
- Financial Meltdown caused by liquidity shortfall in the banking system.
- Housing bust was the step one of the multi-step meltdown.
- Parallel Banking System (Shadow)– Investment banks and hedge funds having important role in financial institutions. Became as important as commercial banks in providing credit to the US Economy. Became a 40% part of the $10 trillion short-term credit market.
- Parallel Banking System relied on credit default swaps to protect themselves against defaults. The largest player on CDSs was AIG. AIG did not have financial strength to handle the onslaught.
- Parallel Banking System drastically cuts short term lending – commercial banks can't meet the needs of US Economy
- Fed starts pumping cash into US Financial Institutions (trillions) including $700 bank bailouts
- US Financial Crisis Inquiry Commission reported findings in Jan 2011:
  1. Crisis was avoidable
  2. Caused by widespread failures in regulations including the Federal Reserve failure to stop toxic mortgages, financial firms taking too much risk, explosive mix of excessive borrowing and risk by households, Wall Street putting the financial system on a collision course, policy makers ill prepared for the crisis, breakdowns in ethics.

This allowed those "banks" to become highly levered—as high as 40 to 1. These entities started lending money not just to the housing market but also to the short-term credit markets where the level of risk expanded dramatically. Regulated commercial banks were not allowed to exceed 10 to 1. This expansion, combined with higher risk, is called financialization.

As soon as the mortgages started to fail, the highly levered investment banks could not withstand the losses. These new lending organizations were part of a new system called the parallel banking system, or what the Democrats call the shadow banking system. By allowing investment banks to have exceptionally high leverage ratios, the federal government made them as large a player in the US economy as traditional commercial banks. By 2006 they were contributing heavily not only into the mortgage market but were a 40 percent player in the

116

short-term credit market. The parallel banking system was heavily using credit default swaps, which were insurance products to ensure that the underlying debt would be paid off. The biggest originator of these CDSs was AIG, who did not have the financial strength to handle a small crisis, much less one as large as the housing market bust. As soon as the mortgages started to fail and the CDSs were found to be worthless, it was discovered that most of the investment banking and hedge funds had tied up most of their liquidity in long-term instruments while short-term instruments were coming due. The chain reaction was failing home mortgages and a drying up of short-term credit in the US economy. In an effort to fix the multiple stupid decisions made by the federal government, President George W. Bush committed to a $700 billion bank bailout, and the Federal Reserve started pumping "cheap money" into banks to refund the short-term credit market. These topics would be discussed in a later class.

John asked Dr. Randolph if he wanted to add anything to the discussion. Randolph added that the reason the investment banks and hedge funds entered into the short-term credit markets was because of their higher rates of return on those investments, as well as a place to "park" excess cash reserves.

John stated that the US Financial Crisis Inquiry Commission issued its findings in January 2011. The first statement was that this crisis was avoidable. John agreed with that statement, but he disagreed with their case on why it was avoidable. If the federal government had not created Fannie Mae and Freddie Mac, had not passed the Community Reinvestment Act of 1977, if Bill Clinton's HUD had not mandated Fannie Mae must make 50 percent of its loans to low- and moderate-income families, and if the SEC had not allowed the five investment banks to run such leverage ratios, this entire situation would have never happened. The financial crisis was caused by the housing market bust; there is no way to get around that. Randolph interjected that deregulation of the banking industry was also a contributing factor. John said he partially agreed; the regulators were too stupid to see what was happening. Housing prices exceeded 10 percent per year growth rates for over a decade. Regulators chose not to regulate CDSs. Finally, the Federal Reserve allowed interest rates to stay abnormally low for too long. Randolph agreed to the premise but felt that greed and unethical behavior were also culprits to the disaster. John also mentioned the repealing of Glass Steagall by Bill Clinton allowed investments banks into traditional commercial banking activities was a significant culprit.

John admitted to the class that while he was chief executive officer of Smith Goldman, he personally made the decision to invest in mortgage-backed securities that were "insured" by CDSs. He also admitted his firm did trade in mortgage-backed securities and issued commercial paper to the short-term credit markets. However, the leverage ratio at the firm never exceeded 15 percent, and the firm did lose money on worthless mortgages and failed CDSs. But the firm did not want to take one dime from the federal government under the TARP program but was forced to by Hank Paulson. The firm repaid every penny with interest as soon as they were allowed to do so. When John retired, the firm was much stronger than when he became CEO many years ago.

He admitted to learning some valuable lessons from the financial disaster. The biggest lesson was that extremely high short-term profits do not beat long-term consistent profits. Randolph added that he has known John for many years and the confession just made was true. The students asked several questions about John's personal experiences. John told them about very candid conversations with Hank Paulson, the secretary of the treasury at that time, and Ben Bernanke, the Federal Reserve chairman. He admitted there were several weekends in the fall of 2008 that everyone was scared that the United States could go into a depression. He personally felt there was no more than a 10 percent chance. The most remarkable aspect of the "forced funding" by Paulson and Bernanke was that the banks did not lend that money into the short-term credit markets. As such, the level of short-term credit remained exceptionally low until 2009. John dismissed the class, and they quietly filed out of the lecture hall.

Randolph walked down the aisle to the front of the lecture hall and shook John's hand. He acknowledged the confession was extremely tough but helpful for the students. John thanked him, and they walked out the lecture hall together.

That night, John shared with Jenny about the class discussion. Jenny was rather surprised John had been so candid during class. John was not sure why he had been so open either. As they cut off the lights, John told Jenny that details behind that confession would probably doom his chances of being a US senator, and Jenny did not disagree.

Chapter 32

On Friday night John and Jenny invited Hank Johnson and several other donors and interested parties to The Willows for dinner. Jenny catered the dinner so that she could also focus on the discussion. Everyone arrived at six thirty. After a few drinks and small talk, the group adjourned to the dining room. Over dinner, John asked Hank several questions about his plan to take the Senate seat away from the Democrats. The strategy was to paint Webb as an Obama loyalist who had voted for ObamaCare and most of the other bills that the progressives offered during the first three years of Obama presidency. The new Democratic candidate would only continue the same voting pattern as Webb. John discussed his time as CEO of Smith Goldman and his experiences during the financial meltdown.

John was straightforward with the group that Obama and Democrats had been quite effective in presenting Wall Street as the bad guy in the housing and financial meltdowns. The group agreed. John asked how much money it would take for him to run a successful campaign. Hank disclosed that Senator Maria Cantwell (D-Washington) stated her re-election campaign could cost $18 million. John and Jenny were dumbfounded. No wonder the country was in such awful shape. Hank continued that in the traditional red state, somewhere between $6 million and $8 million would be enough. John and Jenny thought that was an obscene amount too.

The group went into the front parlor to continue the discussion. Several of the donors asked questions about John's political views. On abortion, John was against it for any reason. John stated that while he is not a woman and could not imagine the complexities in such a decision, the United States should not allow the destruction of a human fetus based on the decision of anyone. On capital punishment, John opposes the death penalty. On gun control, he is against any limitation on guns, including assault weapons. On health care, ObamaCare must be repealed and left to the free market. John continued that Medicare needed to be fixed for those on the program now and later phased out. The federal government needs to get out of the health care business. However, John stated that the country needs tort reform and state-to-state insurance transferability. On immigration, John opposes blanket amnesty for illegal aliens and supports the national identification law passed in Arizona. On stem-cell research, he opposes the use of embryonic stem cells because of their unreliability. On Iraq and Afghanistan, he believes an effective exit plan is needed. John believes the president needs to have a means to fund all military actions. On same-sex marriage, John believes people have a right to do whatever they want to do. However, it is not the responsibility of the federal or state governments to recognize what they are doing. If individual states pass constitutional amendments restricting same sex marriage, it would be in their mandate. The United States Supreme Court does not have any jurisdiction in the matter. John, however, firmly believes that marriage is between a man and a woman. On taxes, John stated that while he hates the idea, the only way the United States is going to balance the budget is a combination of spending cuts and tax increases. John personally believes that there should be 3-to-1 ratio: for every three dollars cut, a dollar can be raised through taxes. He continued that he does not want additional progressive income taxes, but instead either a national sales tax or value-added tax. The first rate would be set by Congress. Any future rate increases would require a two-thirds vote, not 50 percent. On unions, John feels the unions were necessary and vital to the country's early industrial success. Over the last thirty years, unions have become a massive problem to the economy and to the success of the nation. John thinks public unions for teachers and civil service personnel are unconstitutional since the employer—the taxpayer—is not part of the negotiation. John also believes private unions have destroyed prominent companies like General Motors by insisting on inequitable pay and benefits.

Finally, the group had one additional question. What is the most serious problem in the country today? John immediately responded that unemployment is the most pressing issue facing the United States. In addition, the national debt is an overwhelming problem. The national debt is over $14 trillion and has risen by over $4 trillion in the last three years. Obama's ten-year budget has the national debt increasing to over $40 trillion. Even Paul Ryan's ten-year budget has a debt of over $23 trillion. Neither of these plans is acceptable. America needs a plan to be deficit-free in the next three years. In addition, the country needs to have a truly workable plan to eliminate the national debt in the next fifty years. This would require tough choices and some unhappy people. However, someone needs to be the grown-up and not some political hack appeasing everyone to get reelected. John is concerned it may not be possible without:

1. Comprehensive lobbyist reform—Lobbyists on both sides keep any meaningful legislation from getting passed. Only when one side gets a super majority can something like ObamaCare get passed. All lobbyists need to be registered as such. No member of Congress can accept any gifts, money, trips from lobbyist, period. There should be a one-strike-and-you-are-out clause. If one is caught "buying influence," the person is put on a no-contact list that will be published.

2. Term limits for Congress. John stated that it was a disgrace for people to spend thirty, forty and fifty years in Congress. That is not what the founders envisioned. John would like to see no more than three two-year terms for representatives and no more than two four-year terms for senators. This would allow members of Congress to remember that they work for the people of the state and not for themselves.

3. Campaign finance reform. John stated it will take $6 million to $8 million to win a seat in the US Senate that pays $200,000 per year. Ridiculous.

After the discussion, Hank thanked John and Jenny for their hospitality. He told John that he would be an excellent senator for Virginia. John indicated that he was still thinking about it but would make a decision soon.

Chapter 33

On Tuesday morning John walked the sidewalk across from Old Dominion Hall. He and his brother lived in Old Dominion Hall during their senior year. It brought back fond memories. As usual he walked into his office and read some e-mail. There was nothing urgent. At around nine twenty, he walked to the lecture hall. In the back of the room, Randolph nodded to John, who returned the gesture. John put the following slide on the projector:

Session 15 – Bailouts and Stimulus

- Congress approved a $700 billion bailout of banks. Program involved giving banks money (through issuance of preferred stock)
- Intent was to increase the amount of short-term capital and to stabilize the financial markets
- Called the "Troubled Asset Relief Program" or TARP.
- The Treasury required all banks to take part (whether they wanted the money or not).
- The concept of "too big to fail" was used extensively by Bush and Obama
- The bailout allowed the federal government to decide the winners and losers --

Winners	Losers
Auto Unions	Auto Stockholders
Goldman Sachs	Auto Debtholders
AIG	Bear Sterns
Some Taxpayers	Lehman Bros

John proposed that as the housing market burst and the short-term credit markets dried up, the country faced a situation remarkably similar but in many ways decidedly different than the Great Depression. The Great Depression was started by the 1929 stock market crash, but the real problem causing the Great Depression was no short-term credit availability. As soon as that happened, there was a "run on the bank." Bank customers went to the bank to retrieve their money, but there was not enough to go around. The banking system does not have 100 percent of the money each person has in the system. Hank Paulson, who was the former head of Goldman Sachs and the current secretary of the treasury, was truly concerned that another Great Depression could occur. Lehman Brothers, the fourth largest investment banking firm, went bankrupt, and Bear Sterns was sold at a bargain to JP Morgan. Merrill Lynch and Goldman Sachs were probably frightfully close to bankruptcy as people started withdrawing money out of their institutions.

Over a thirty-day period in September and October 2008, Hank Paulson convinced President Bush, Congress, and the heads of the country's big banks that the second Great Depression was coming. Paulson "required" each bank to sell nonvoting preferred stock to the federal government for cash. He believed that the banks would use this money to start lending again, specifically in the short-term credit markets. Goldman Sachs sold a portion of their stock to Warren Buffett, and Hank Paulson bullied Bank of America into purchasing Merrill Lynch. Hank Paulson and Ben Bernanke stated the $700 billion was needed because these financial entities were "too big to fail." After Barack Obama became president, the program was extended to both General Motors and Chrysler, both of which were almost bankrupt. This action was wrong because TARP was for increasing the amount of liquidity in the financial markets, not bailing out companies that were mismanaged. The top twenty recipients of money were as follows:

Session 15 – Bailouts and Stimulus

	Name	Amount Disbursed	Amount Repaid
1	Fannie Mae	98,700	-
2	AIG	67,835	9,146
3	Freddie Mac	63,700	-
4	General Motors	50,745	22,828
5	Bank of America	45,000	45,000
6	Citigroup	45,000	45,000
7	JP Morgan Chase	25,000	25,000
8	Wells Fargo	25,000	25,000
9	GMAC (Ally Financial)	16,290	2,667
10	Chrysler	12,812	2,180
11	Goldman Sachs	10,000	10,000
12	Morgan Stanley	10,000	10,000
13	PNC Financial Services	7,579	7,579
14	US Bancorp	6,599	6,599
15	SunTrust	4,850	4,850
16	Capital One Financial Group	3,555	3,555
17	Regions Financial Corp	3,500	-
18	Fifth Third Bancorp	3,408	3,408
19	Hartford Financial Group	3,400	3,400
20	American Express	3,389	3,389

- US will never get money back from Fannie and Freddie – losses are going to be higher
- AIG will never pay back entire amount
- GM and Chrysler will take many years to payback
- Bank of America was "forced" by Paulson and Bernanke to purchase Merrill Lynch

Did it work?
No. Banks did not lend the money and the short-term credit remained tight until 2009.

Source: Wall Street Journal

John stated the big banks had repaid their amounts in full as of today. Fannie and Freddie both owed 100 percent of their funds taken, and the taxpayers will have additional losses as the toxic assets are found. AIG has made little progress. GM and Chrysler also owe quite a bit more. John asked the class if TARP worked. It did not. The banks did not lend the money, and the short-term credit market remained tight until 2009.

John stated that Paulson will go down as one of the worst treasury secretaries of all time. He was in the wrong place at the wrong time, but part of the problem was his own doing. TARP was a complete failure, and it allowed the federal government to temporarily "nationalize" the US banking industry. It also allowed the federal government to pick winners and losers. The biggest loser is the American taxpayer, who will have to repay the sins of Freddie and Fannie, AIG, and potentially GM and Chrysler.

GM's and Chrysler's stockholders and debt-holders received nothing. The unions walked away with 33 percent of the respective companies (it pays to support the right guy at election time). AIG management should have been put in jail for the fraud they committed. Every taxpayer who benefited from selling their real estate at profits greater than 4 percent per annum was also a winner.

John asked Randolph if he had any thoughts to add. Randolph added that politicians from both parties also walked off "scot-free." John agreed.

John put the next slide on the projector:

Session 15 – Bailouts and Stimulus

- In an effort to move the economy out of recession, President Obama proposed a $790 billion "stimulus" package to ensure that unemployment doesn't go higher than 8.2%
- Spending increases comprised $311 billion, tax cuts comprised $301 billion, and aid comprised $178 billion.
- Opinion – largest waste of money in the history of the world

	Stimulate	Pork	Welfare
Spending	$ 22,343	$ 227,776	$ 61,220
Tax Cuts	$ 28,284	$ 25,887	$ 246,964
Aid	$ -	$ 22,772	$ 155,368
Total	$ 50,627	$ 276,435	$ 463,552
Grand Total			$ 790,614

- The pork spending was heavily given to progessive liberal causes
- The $790 billion didn't improve the economy and didn't keep unemployment from soaring to 9.8%.
- Again the federal government overstepped its Constitutional authority

---

He pointed out that the combination of the housing bust and financial meltdown put the country into a recession. In terms of the recession, it was not the worst since the Great Depression, as Obama has stated on many occasions (the 1982 recession was worse). When unemployment reached 7 percent, Obama, using a lot of the goodwill from the election, petitioned Congress for a massive $787 billion stimulus bill. America had never seen such a large measure to shore up the country. Obama promised, if the stimulus was passed, unemployment would not exceed 8.2 percent (it went to 9.8 percent). The bill was a combination of additional spending of $311 billion, targeted tax cuts of $301 billion, and aid, primarily to states of $178 billion. John stated, in his opinion, it was the single largest waste of money in the history of the United States. He went through every line of spending and found only $50 million was truly stimulus. The majority of the bill was welfare such as additional unemployment benefits, bailing out states with deficits, additional money (not tax benefits) for low- and lower-middle-class people, and $250 per person for retirees. The rest, John believed, was pork. High-speed rails, green projects, funding research, grants to arts, and science projects. Complete waste of money for a country that cannot pay their bills.

Randolph pointed out that some of this was opinion. The recession could have been more severe. John countered it could have rebounded in the same manner with no stimulus. Who really knows? The issue is massive spending without any concrete, tangible, and measurable benefits. That, by definition, is waste. John continued that the recovery from this recession is the weakest on record. If one puts two and two together, one has to acknowledge this stimulus was a failure. Randolph reasoned the financial meltdown and housing bust made this event different from every other recession, lasting longer than any other one. John retorted that if Obama would have used different means, the result would have been different. Throwing money at a problem does not fix it, as seen by the Department of Education. John concluded by noting that Congress and the president again overstepped their Constitutional authority by agreeing to this stimulus.

John stated that starting in 2006 through today, the US economy has gone through a necessary correction caused by many poor decisions and reckless behavior. The creation of Fannie/Freddie, the Community Reinvestment Act, and the subsequent increases to that legislation, granting investment banks the ability to engage in commercial bank activities without holding them to leverage ratios, and holding the discount rate at historic low amounts for long periods of time were errors made by the federal government. People who want to stay in power for longer periods of time can cause lots of damage.

Americans purchasing homes they could not afford with little or no down payment money made poor decisions bordering on reckless. Commercial banks changed their lending practices to allow mortgages for people with credit scores lower than 620 and without 20 percent down. Investment banks that allowed their leverage ratios to exceed acceptable amounts were careless. AIG allowing itself to be the biggest player in the CDS arena without the means to properly assess the overall risk was downright criminal. John stated it was his belief the recession will continue, and housing prices will continue to decline. Randolph did not disagree.

John concluded by saying that next session would touch upon one of the most heinous pieces of legislation in the history of the United States—ObamaCare. There was the familiar frown on Randolph's face.

Chapter 34

On Wednesday John prepared his lesson for Thursday's class. He went to the college to escape from his looming decision of whether to run for Senate. He was concerned about the media prying that would take place in his and Jenny's personal lives. He was also questioning whether he could actually win the election. He was also concerned about the change in lifestyle, going from a peaceful existence to one of constant campaigning. He was concerned about failing to accomplish all of his goals if he were fortunate enough to be elected. There was a great deal to ponder.

John looked up when there was a knock on his door. It was one of his students from class, Stephanie Norris. John invited her into the office and offered her a seat. She asked him for more details relating to his days at Smith Goldman. Specifically, she wanted to know how the decision of trading mortgage-backed securities affected the firm.

John responded that profits increased dramatically, and people reaped enormous bonuses. He admitted he would not let the firm go "too deep" with these instruments. He did not take part in the real low-end tranches that were so lucrative for many of the investment banking firms. He admitted he was highly skeptical about AIG's credit default swaps, and he also admitted that he failed to see the upcoming housing market bust. He revealed that when he saw it beginning, he started writing down the riskier tranche positions. Stephanie asked if the firm fired any people due to these events. John regretfully admitted there were some headcount reductions, but less than 5 percent of the total workforce. Stephanie told John that her father used to work for Lehman Brothers in New York. She remembers the days leading up to firm's bankruptcy and how depressed her father was. Her mother was extremely angry at Wall Street. She did not understand at the time but now has a better understanding of what happened and why it happened. She asked if John was a Republican. He revealed he was a conservative and agreed more with the Republican Party than the Democrats.

John asked Stephanie if her father found a new job. She joyfully said he has a job now that he loves at Bank of America (formerly Merrill Lynch). John was relieved to hear this fantastic news. Stephanie thanked John for his time in answering her questions. John reflected it was easy to get caught up in who was to blame and why it happened. The real tragedy is what happened to innocent people, whether it was people who lost their jobs or their homes. The conversation had an impact on John as he replayed it in his mind the rest of the day. He kept coming back to whether or not he could make a real difference in the US economy as a senator from Virginia.

Chapter 35

John walked into class at nine twenty-five a.m. on Thursday and looked around the room. William Randolph was not there, and the class was already seated for the discussion. John put the following slide on the projector:

Session 26 - ObamaCare

- In December 2009, Obama and the Democrats in Congress passed ObamaCare
- Holy Grail for Progressives and something that had been sought since FDR
- Most Americans do not want this government takeover of healthcare.
- Facts and Figures
  1. 32 million new people will be insured
  2. $940 billion is the estimated cost over 10 years
  3. $29 thousand for each new person covered
  4. $88 thousand and lower for family of 4 would received federal subsidy
  5. Age 26 – Employers would have to cover dependents through age 26
  6. 40% Tax on insurance companies providing Cadillac health plans
  7. 3.8% Medicare Tax on investment income
  8. $695 or 2.5% - fine if you don't have coverage
  9. 50 employees – companies with over 50 employees would have to $2 thousand per worker if don't have coverage
  10. 0.9% Medicare Part A would be increased to 2.35%
  11. $16 billion would be paid by drug manufacturers
  12. $47 billion would be paid by health insurance providers
  13. 2.9% Excise tax on medical device manufacturers
  14. $132 billion reduced payments to Medicare Advantage
  15. Flexible Spending account reduced from $5k to $2.5k

John asked for a show of hands on how many remember Congress passing ObamaCare in December 2009. Just about everyone in class raised their hands. John asked them to state their opinion on ObamaCare, and its potential impact on America. About 25 percent of the students thought it positive for America, 25 percent said it was the wrong decision for America, and the rest of the class withheld judgment. John continued by saying that government run health care has been the desire of progressive liberals since LBJ introduced Medicare and

Medicaid in the 1960s. Most polls still reveal Americans are not in favor of ObamaCare. One student asked why John refers to the health-care reform as ObamaCare. He responded that according to David Axelrod, it was the primary goal for Obama and his administration. Another student asked how it could be wrong for an additional thirty-two million without health-care insurance to have coverage. John replied the bill had nothing to do with health care in the United States but everything to do with control. If the goal was to get coverage for the thirty-two million uninsured people, all Congress had to do was change Medicaid rules to include them. Let's look at the facts, not the hype:

1. Thirty-two million new people will be covered at an additional cost of $940 billion over the first ten years, according to the Congressional Budget Office. That is only $3,000 per year. The math does not make sense when most employers are paying around $30,000 per year per employee (not including the employee's portion). The truth is that the first three years of the new reform will have revenues coming in and no expenses being paid. The true cost will be around $2 trillion, on a conservative basis, for the first ten years.

2. The reform act sets a floor on who is eligible for subsidies—families of four making $88,000.

3. Employers would have to cover employees' children through age twenty-six. This will require companies to assess hiring and firing people.

4. Forty percent surtax on companies offering Cadillac insurance plans—a waiver given to the auto unions already.

5. A Medicare tax of 3.8 percent on all investment income (the taxpayer will have to pay both the employer's and employee's part). This includes proceeds on the sale of home.

6. If one elects not to have insurance, one will have to pay $695 per month to the federal government as a fine. This is unconstitutional.

7. Employers with more than fifty employees must pay $2,000 per employee. Waiver granted to McDonald's.

8. A total of $132 billion taken out of Medicare Advantage program and moved to this new health-care program.

John pointed out these are just some of the heinous parts of this bill. One student responded that President Obama said that this reform act would control costs. John replied if President Obama was so concerned about controlling costs, why did not he insert language to have true tort reform. John put up the second slide:

- Winners and Losers – Winners – McDonalds, Auto Unions, Waiver Grantees
- Taxes start in 2011, while the first benefit will be paid out in 2014 or 2015. True 10 year cost is closer to $2 trillion.
- Requiring people to take insurance or be fined is unconstitutional
- Lower federal and state courts have ruled this bill to be unconstitutional
- Many state Attorney Generals have sued the federal government
- A true healthcare reform would have dealt with Tort Reform – malpractice insurance can be up to 25% of a doctor's cost
- 2010 Mid Term Elections showed how unpopular this law is.

The government can not give something to someone unless it takes it from someone else.

He continued saying malpractice insurance to keep lawyers at bay comprises 25 percent of doctors' overall costs. That means health-care costs could have dropped by 25 percent if there was true tort reform. Finally, one student asked if health care is a right for Americans. John rhetorically asked where that right is enumerated in the Constitution. President Obama and the progressives have done a superb job of explaining that health care is a basic right. It is not. It is not any more of a right than owning a car, a house, or having a job. This health-care reform bill:

1. Steals from seniors ($132 billion out of Medicare Advantage Program)

2. Requires everyone in America to purchase medical insurance or be fined

3. Continues to increase taxes

4. Picks liberal winners and losers—any person or company granted a waiver is a winner, everyone else will be a loser in the end

John suggested that the United States has the best medical system in the world. That is why countries with socialized medicine often have their citizens come to the United States for treatment. How many new drugs are created in Canada or the United Kingdom? None. Nearly every new life saving drug is created in the United States.

There needs to be changes to the current health-care system after repealing ObamaCare. Tort reform should have been the first thing passed by Congress, but it was not because trial lawyers are heavy contributors to the Democratic party. Insurance policies should be portable—able to be used from state to state. Currently, insurance companies are regulated by individual states, and tend to contribute heavily to Republican candidates.

John continued that one may argue that the bill just needs to be changed, as opposed to repealing the entire bill. The Democrats made that impossible. There is a provision in the bill saying that nothing can be removed without killing the entire bill. The Democrats thought they were being smart, but at the end of the day, the provision will cause the entire bill to be repealed. John's opinion was that the requirement that everyone must have insurance will be deemed unconstitutional by the Supreme Court, and the bill will be repealed.

At the end of the day, ObamaCare was a bill for the control of the health-care system. Do not be fooled that it was something other than that. John again asked the students to express opinions on whether the health-care reform bill was the right thing for the United States. The original 25 percent who favored the bill were still in favor. About 75 percent of the group that was noncommittal was now against the bill. Based on the final tally, this class represents the mood of the country. John closed with the following statement: *The government cannot give something to someone without first taking it from someone else.* John thanked the class for the discussion.

Chapter 36

John and Jenny had the grandchildren over Friday night for a sleepover. As soon as the grandchildren arrived at The Willows, they changed and jumped in the pool. Jenny watched them as they splashed and kicked around in the water. They begged John to get in, but the water was too chilly for him in April. He asked them what they wanted for dinner, and in unison they screamed, "Cheeseburgers, fries, and ice cream." John went to the grocery store to get the necessary provisions.

After dinner and baths for all, everyone went down to the basement for time in the movie room. The grandchildren picked a movie, and they watched together. At around ten o'clock, Jenny announced that it was time for bed as a collective groan was bellowed. John and Jenny tucked the grandchildren in bed, and they retired to their bedroom. They talked about John's running for office for easily two hours. There were a lot of negatives, but there were some positives. Jenny asked the key question of whether or not John wanted to do it. John just did not know.

John awoke at about four thirty a.m. and went to his home office. He read some e-mail and looked at the Internet. He prayed about the decision but was not hearing from God. He decided to go for a walk as the sun was coming up. John loved The Willows and could not imagine leaving it again for long periods of time. However, John did feel a sense of duty to the country. He worried he may not have enough influence as "just a senator."

At around seven thirty, John walked back up to the house. Jenny was up and watching him as he walked to the back door. She asked where he had been as he walked into the kitchen. He explained to her where he had been and what he was thinking. She encouraged him to continue to pray about it and eventually God would direct his path. As soon as their discussion concluded, the grandchildren came running en masse down the steps looking for food. Jenny prepared chocolate chip pancakes while John poured orange juice. Everyone enjoyed breakfast, as always. After breakfast, everyone walked down to the horse pasture. The grandchildren asked for horse rides, which John obliged. In the late afternoon, John's and Jenny's children joined the group for baby back ribs that John had started in the smoker earlier in the day. The outside temperature was around eighty-five degrees, and the grandchildren talked the adults into swimming. Everyone left around nine thirty, and John and Jenny fell into bed. It was an exciting but very tiring day.

On Sunday John and Jenny went to church and took the family out to lunch afterward. They spent the rest of Sunday discussing the future.

Chapter 37

On Tuesday morning John arrived at the office at about eight thirty a.m. and read some e-mail. There was one from Hank Johnson asking a very straightforward question: "Your decision?"

John responded he would call later in the day. He walked to the lecture hall and was greeted by a couple of his students. He noticed that Randolph was back in his regular seat. They exchanged smiles, and John continued in his preparation for class. He put the following slide on the projector:

Session 27 – Who Owns America?

Percentage of US Treasuries Owned by Foreigners

Year	%
1994	19.0%
2003	46.0%
2004	51.0%
2005	52.0%
2006	52.0%
2007	57.0%
2008	61.0%
2009	57.0%

Country	USD (bill)	% of All
China	1,155	26%
Japan	886	20%
Oil countrie	216	5%
Brazil	198	4%
Russia	139	3%
All Others	1,861	42%

Source: wikipedia.org

John started by pointing out that before 2000, the amount of the debt held by foreign countries was less than 20 percent. Starting in 2000, which was the first year that China started as a true economic power, the percentage went to 35 percent and has risen to more than 50 percent. China currently holds 26 percent of US debt, Japan holds 20 percent, and oil-producing countries hold another 5 percent. That comprises of more than half of the United States' outstanding debt. Even Russia, the United States' biggest enemy before the end of the Cold War, owns 3 percent. It is a truly concerning situation.

John asked what would happen if China decided to "dump" its holdings on the open market. The students thought it would be a complete travesty. John disagreed and said if China did that, it would be more harmful to China than the United States. Randolph stated that if China dumped their holdings, the US dollar would fail. John agreed but said that China would lose any chance of collecting 100 percent of the outstanding debt. John asked what would happen if Japan started to systematically reduce its holdings. He continued by saying the Japanese population was aging and would need money for retirees. The students were not sure. A gradual reduction in debt holdings would not be significant. However, it may require additional interest if the debt was not gobbled up by other countries.

John presented the following slide:

Richest Americans		Largest Landowners	
	In Billions		In Millions of Acres
Bill Gates	54.0	US Government	728.8
Warren Buffet	45.0	Ted Turner	2.0
Larry Ellison	27.0	Red Emmerson	1.7
Christy Walton	24.0	Brad Kelley	1.7
Charles Koch	21.5	Irving Family	1.2
David Koch	21.5	John Malone	1.2
Jim Walton	20.1	Singleton Family	1.1
Alice Walton	20.0	King Ranch	0.9
Robson Walton	19.7	Pingree Heirs	0.8
Michael Bloomberg	18.0	Reed Family	0.8
		Stan Kroenke	0.7

Source: Forbes Magazine 2010   Source: The Wall Street Journal 2010

The left side of the slide showed the richest people in the United States. The right side showed the country's largest landowners. John pointed out that the United States government is by far the largest landowner in the country. The government owning land began with President Ulysses Grant when he took the land comprising Yellowstone National Park. John also suggested governmental land ownership is unconstitutional. Several of the students stated that US national parks are some of the best in the world. John agreed, but pointed out that the Constitution did not allow for land ownership by the federal government. He asked why the founders did not want the federal government to own land directly. There were no responses from the class. The colonists had just freed themselves from a king (federal government) who owned all of the land. They would have never allowed the federal government to do the same thing. He asked what the class thought about selling some of the land to pay off the debt. The students liked the idea. John revealed that selling 100 million acres at $10,000 per acre would bring in $1 trillion. If the federal government sold all of its land, the national debt could be cut in half.

John asked the class to think about who owns America. Do the debt holders, the richest Americans, or the landowners own the country? Americans own America. Each vote carries the same weight as the next vote. Each of us owns America. Politicians will say otherwise; do not ever agree with them.

Chapter 38

William Randolph followed John back to his office. They discussed the concept of ownership of the country for about an hour.

John asked Randolph if he had ever considered leaving the college to pursue something else. Randolph revealed that he had on many occasions, but always talked himself out of it. John asked him if he would consider at least a leave of absence if the right opportunity came along. Randolph tried to glean more information on what John was thinking, but John would not reveal anything for a couple of days. John invited Randolph for golf on Saturday afternoon, and they agreed to meet at Ford's Colony at around one o'clock.

John telephoned Hank Johnson. He asked if he could come to The Willows on Thursday night. John had made a decision, but it was not one of the choices on the table. At home he and Jenny continued discussing the upcoming decision. Jenny knew that John had always been interested in politics, but secretly she was not thrilled about this conclusion. She also knew that once John made up his mind, it was a lost cause in convincing him otherwise. They talked about what it would mean in their lives. In the end, Jenny did not want to admit it, but it was exciting.

They went to bed that night still discussing the ramifications of the decision. Neither slept well as anticipation was mounting. The next morning John and Jenny went out for breakfast. By the end of the day, they had come to a complete resolution, and were ready to make the announcement.

Chapter 39

John walked into the lecture hall at nine twenty a.m. He looked up and smiled at Randolph and put the following slide on the projector:

Session 28 – Runaway Spending			
(in billions USDs)	Obama's Feb-11 Budget for FY 2012	Ryan's Apr-11 Budget for FY 2012	Difference
Expected GDP	15,797.1	15,684.4	112.7
Receipts:			
Individual income taxes	1,141.0		
Corporate income taxes	329.0		
Social security payroll taxes	659.0		
Medicare payroll taxes	201.0		
Unemployment insurance	57.0		
Other retirement	8.0		
Excise taxes	103.0		
Estate and gift taxes	14.0		
Customs and duties	30.0		
Federal Reserve earnings	66.0		
Other miscellaneous receipts	20.0		
Total receipts	2,628.0	2,533.0	95.0
Outlays:			
Discretionary Spending			
Security	884.0	801.0	83.0
Non-Security	456.0	482.0	(26.0)
Total Discretionary	1,340.0	1,283.0	57.0
Mandatory Spending			
Social Security	761.0	760.0	1.0
Medicare	485.0	560.0	(75.0)
Medicaid	269.0	259.0	10.0
TARP	13.0	-	13.0
Other Mandatory programs	612.0	410.0	202.0
Total Mandatory Spending	2,140.0	1,989.0	151.0
Interest	242.0	256.0	(14.0)
Disaster Costs	6.0	-	6.0
Total Outlays	3,728.0	3,528.0	200.0
Deficit	(1,100.0)	(995.0)	(105.0)

John stated that President Obama's 2012 budget called for a deficit of $1.1 trillion. Paul Ryan's 2012 budget called for a deficit of just under $1.0 trillion. He asked the class for discussion on how either of these budgets can be acceptable to the American people. Most students commented that the budgets were not acceptable. What is equally disturbing is that the revenue projections are probably overstated. John showed the next slide.

	Revenues	Spending	Deficit	Debt
Session 28 – Runaway Spending				
Beginning				5,911
Clinton 2000	2,026	1,789	236	5,674
Bush 2001	1,991	2,125	(134)	5,808
Bush 2002	1,853	2,273	(420)	6,228
Bush 2003	1,783	2,338	(555)	6,783
Bush 2004	1,880	2,476	(596)	7,379
Bush 2005	2,154	2,708	(554)	7,933
Bush 2006	2,407	2,981	(574)	8,507
Bush 2007	2,568	3,069	(501)	9,008
Bush 2008	2,524	3,502	(978)	9,986
Obama 2009	2,108	3,520	(1,412)	11,398
Obama 2010	2,163	3,456	(1,293)	12,691
Obama 2011	2,174	3,819	(1,645)	14,336

Source: www.usgovernmentspending.com

John stated that since Obama had taken office, spending has increased by 28 percent while tax revenues have been flat at around $2.1 trillion per year. John wondered why people are not protesting in the streets about this matter. Randolph agreed that spending was a serious problem, but believes that some of the spending averted a potential depression. John disagreed. The largest dollar increase was in defense. How did that prevent a depression? The increases in health care and pensions did not prevent a depression. The truth of the matter is President Obama has not executed the correct policies to stop this runaway spending. John stated that Moody's rating agency has threatened to downgrade US debt. If that happens, interest rates will have to rise on the debt, and the interest that we pay will increase accordingly. The Federal Reserve is printing money, thus driving down the value of the US dollar against foreign currencies.

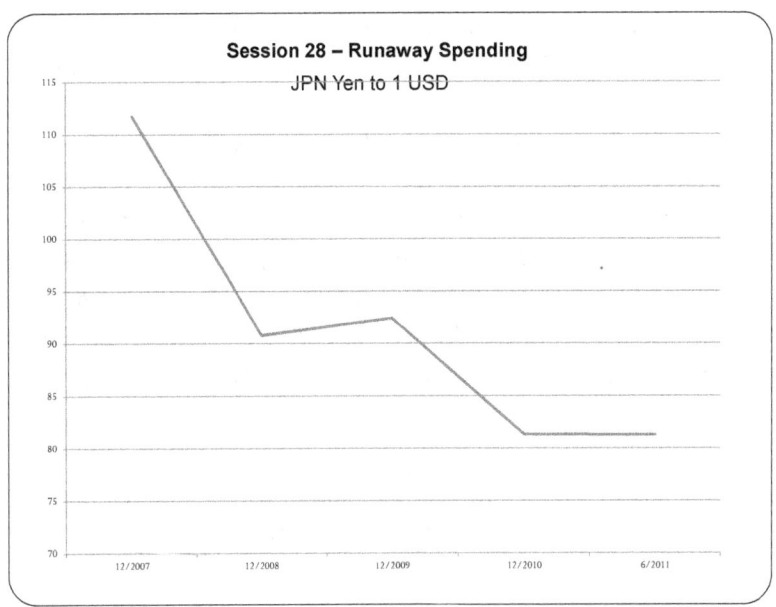

Session 28 – Runaway Spending
JPN Yen to 1 USD

John pointed out that the US dollar has weakened against the Japanese yen, Canadian dollar, Singapore dollar, and even the Mexican peso since spending has increased. The euro has been moving inconsistently due to the debt problems in Europe.

John continued by saying that runaway spending and running up massive deficits is destroying the value of the dollar. This will have significant unfavorable impacts on American's buying power. Eventually, the dollar will be no more valuable than any other currency, and the US dollar will lose its status as the "world's reserve currency." Currently, most economic transactions use the US dollar as the primary currency. If that changes, the United States' importance in the world economy will diminish.

John told the students that the next class would be the last class in the semester. The subject matter would be how to fix the US economy. John said he would present a blueprint he has developed over the last couple of years. He wanted the class to understand that it was one man's opinion. To truly fix the economy, many ideas are needed to formulate a successful plan. Time is running out for US economic power on the world stage unless changes are made quickly. John told the class that he would like them to think about how they would change the US economy for the better.

John went home to collect his thoughts before meeting with Hank Johnson that night.

Chapter 40

Jenny prepared finger foods for the meeting, and John helped her with the last minute details and preparations. Promptly at seven o'clock, the doorbell rang.

John opened the door and Hank smiled and said, "How's it going, Mr. Senator."

John smiled and invited Hank into the living room off the main hallway. The men poured themselves a drink and sat down. The tension was extremely thick.

John thanked Hank for coming over and for the wonderful opportunity of potentially becoming a senator for Virginia. John pointed out that things in America have eroded over the last three to four years to a place where radical changes are needed. Spending is out of control, the deficits, and amount of debt are growing faster than when the United States was fighting in World War II. Entitlements have become a way of life, as opposed to a means of helping someone out, and the world is in turmoil with the Middle East revolts. John felt a true sense of duty, almost a calling, to do something for America, which had afforded him so many incredible opportunities. John told Hank that he and Jenny had discussed this on just about every level imaginable and collectively had made a decision.

Impatiently, Hank asked, "What is your decision?"

John answered, "Hank, I would like you to help me become the president of the United States."

The silence in the room was deafening. Both John and Jenny looked directly at Hank, who sat there speechless. After about thirty uncomfortable seconds, John told Hank that he wanted him to be his campaign manager. Hank looked directly at John but was speechless. John said he knew this was a complete shock, but he has a plan to fix the economy and a plan to heal a lot of the problems facing America. John restated that he needed Hank's help in getting elected president.

Hank pointed out that John had no political experience, was not known by the American people, and did not have an organization. John agreed with all of the points but countered that the United States needs someone with business acumen to run this country. The people do not need a candidate that has an organization but instead has the support and trust of average Americans. Hank revealed one needs at least $500 million to win the presidency. John stated that he was going to put up the first $100 million himself. This statement made Hank realize that this was real—not just someone talking, but someone putting up a substantial sum to do what they thought was right. For every unfavorable reason that Hank could muster, John had a valid and justifiable counter.

John looked at Hank and said we are almost at the end of April 2011. For the campaign to succeed, John needed to announce his intentions within the next couple of months. After the announcement, John would need to spend considerable time in Iowa and New Hampshire. John needed to build a grassroots effort of people to get behind him and to start the ball rolling. He told Hank that he needed him and his vast experience for a successful campaign.

"This will not work without you," John said.

Hank stood up and said he needed to think about it for a while. John understood. They shook hands before Hank left with much to consider.

Chapter 41

On Saturday morning John looked forward to playing golf with William Randolph. Even though they disagreed on a lot of political issues, the men enjoyed each other's company. They met at Ford's Colony and teed off around one twenty-five. It was an enjoyable round. But as usual Randolph won the match. As they were unloading the golf cart, John asked Randolph to call his wife and join them at The Willows for a steak. John also mentioned he had something hugely important to discuss with both of them. Randolph pulled out his cell phone and called his wife. After a very brief conversation, he said he would go home, collect his wife, and drive right over.

On the way to The Willows, John called Jenny and told her that Randolph and his wife were coming to dinner. Jenny asked if he had asked him the question. John said he would ask over dinner. Jenny pulled four steaks out of the freezer so they would defrost. John got home and started pacing. He was nervous about the upcoming conversation.

William and Sarah Randolph knocked on the door around seven o'clock. John rushed to the door, happily greeted them, and invited them into the house. As usual, Jenny hugged both William and Sarah. William and John poured a drink and walked out on the patio where John was preparing the grill for cooking. Abruptly, John looked at William and told him that he was going to run for president of the United States. William looked at John in complete disbelief and burst out laughing. He looked at John, who was not smiling or laughing. He asked if this was a joke.

"Why would you run for President?" William inquired.

John said that he felt a calling to do this, and he had a plan to fix the economy, a plan to fix the many problems that were facing America, a plan to put America back on the right track. William stood there in disbelief. John looked directly at William and said he needed him to make this work. He asked William to be his chief of staff. John said he asked Hank Johnson to be his campaign manager. He reiterated that he needed William to join him to win. William reminded him that they disagree on a lot of issues. John pointed out that the individual parties had just about ruined America. America needs people coming together to find solutions, not just playing politics. William said that was an unusually naïve statement. He continued that the government is politics. William knew more about politics than John would ever know, and that is why John needed William as his chief of staff.

Jenny and Sarah walked out on the patio. William announced to Sarah that John must be crazy. John looked directly at Sarah and said that he was running for president, had asked William to be his chief of staff, and could not win without him. Sarah's mouth dropped. The rest of the evening was a free-for-all with exceptionally loud discussions. Not much food was eaten that night. John presented to both William and Sarah his plan for fixing America. William and John debated some of the items in the plan, and the men flatly disagreed on some of the points. The discussion went late into the night and at around midnight, William and Sarah left The Willows. William promised John that Sarah and he would think about the offer and get back to him. John and Jenny wondered what their decision would be.

Chapter 42

John entered the lecture hall at around 9:25 on the final day of class. He was sad to close this chapter of his life and wanted to end the class on a big note. He hoped that the students had seen "the other side" of the story and perhaps a few of them had changed their opinions. He put the following slide on the projector:

Session 29 – How to Fix America
Nine-Point Plan

The Critical Three

- Comprehensive Lobbyist Reform
- Campaign Finance Reform
- Term Limits for Congress

The Big Six

- Entitlement Programs Reform
- Health Insurance Reform
- Earmarks and Spending
- Disband Department of Education
- Disband Public Unions
- Modify and Simplify the Tax Code

He began by saying that the United States has a lot of problems. The economy is not healthy. The country has too much debt and spends more than it brings into the treasury. There are significant disagreements on health-care reform, illegal immigration, unions, bailouts, and stimulus spending. On the world front, the Middle East is in turmoil as countries are revolting against their leaders, and leaders are killing innocent people. The United States

157

is still fighting in Afghanistan and Iraq and has committed troops in other parts of the world. Islamic terrorists continue to threaten the lives of Americans.

John proposed that the best America is a strong America. The United States needs to fix itself. However, there are three changes that have to happen before any real change can take place. First, Congress needs to pass comprehensive lobbyist reforms. The concept of "buying influence" needs to be a thing in the past. There should be no money passed from lobbyists to members of Congress—period. Secondly, the country needs campaign finance reform. President Obama spent more than $700 million to get elected in 2008. There are some people estimating it will take over $1 billion to defeat him in 2012. This is ridiculous. Congress needs to eliminate all "soft" money funneled into campaigns. Finally, a constitutional amendment needs to be passed to have term limits for Congress. It is utterly absurd for a person to spend decades in Congress. John concluded by saying once these three legislative steps have been taken, the United States can start fixing its problems.

He continued by presenting "the big six" points of his plan. The first areas that need to be addressed are entitlement and mandatory spending programs. These programs have been increasing at unsustainable rates over the last twenty years. John admits fixing these programs will be extremely unpopular, but someone needs to be the adult and shift the country into awareness and discussion about this. He also stated ObamaCare needs to be repealed immediately.

The second area is to have true health-care reform. This would include tort reform, interstate insurance transferability, changing the concept of insurance, elimination of ineffective regulations, and making it easier to create drugs. The key is to fix what we have, and not eliminate the world's best medical system to create another.

Third, Congress needs new guidelines on taxing, spending, and earmarks. John stated earmarks should be eliminated immediately. The new spending and taxing guidelines would require confirmation from the Congressional Budget Office that such measures were self-sustaining. The guidelines would include the development and implementation of a plan to balance the budget, and Congress and the president would have the same retirement and health-care programs as the rest of the country.

Fourth, the Department of Education must be disbanded and put at the state level. In order to have consistent standards, a non-compensated board of state educators would be elected to serve as an advisory committee to set goals and standards for the country.

Fifth, all public unions should be disbanded. John stated that these organizations should be considered illegal. In private companies, union personnel negotiate with the owners or proxies of the owners. In public unions, one union member is negotiating with another union member. This practice should be disbanded immediately.

Sixth, the tax code needs to be gutted and replaced with a flat tax system with lower tax rates. This would eliminate all deductions and make the system truly progressive, as opposed to the system today based on whose lobbyist has more influence.

John asked the students what they thought. Most of the students sat silently thinking about the plan. A couple of students said they liked the plan. There were some who voiced concerns on changes to the entitlement programs. All in all, it was favorably received. John handed out a paper called "How to Fix America."

At the end of class, John announced that Doctor Randolph would administer the final examination a week from Wednesday. He told them that it had been a joy teaching this course and getting to know some of the students and hear their thoughts. John thanked them for their contributions and wished them well during the upcoming examination season.

Chapter 43

Jenny had invited their children and grandchildren over for dinner on Tuesday night. The children had spoken with each other about how unusual a weeknight dinner was, but they concluded that it was probably nothing. Jenny had made Mrs. Mackey's Chicken, a dish in which stuffing mix is used to coat the chicken. It was one of the all-time favorites. After dinner, John and Jenny said they had some news that would affect all of them.

John stated that he loved this family more than anything else in the world. He said that Jenny and he have enjoyed being so close for the past six months. John also stated he loved America, but America has a lot of problems. Problems are not being fixed, and the economy continues to be exceedingly weak. John stated he would announce his candidacy for president tomorrow at the Wren Building at eleven a.m. The children sat there stunned. Finally after some tense moments, they started discussing what impact this news may have on the family. John reminded them that his chances for winning were probably slim. But he felt a need to get out and try to make things better for the country. At the end of the evening, the children hugged their parents and told them that they were proud of their decision. They would be at the Wren Building no later than ten thirty with the grandchildren for the announcement.

Chapter 44

John and Jenny arrived at the Wren Building at ten thirty a.m. As they strolled up the brick sidewalk, the children and grandchildren greeted them in their Sunday's best. John saw Hank running around making last minute changes. He noticed a podium at the top of the steps facing the Capitol on Duke of Gloucester Street. On the podium, a placard read "We Can Fix America." John liked it. He noticed a couple of television camera crews, including WAVY channel 7. He also noticed Thornton Smith, president of the college, walking toward him. John greeted him warmly and thanked him for allowing him to make the announcement on campus. Smith said he would do anything for an alumnus.

At about eleven o'clock, Hank walked up the steps and took his place behind the podium. He thanked everyone who had come, and introduced John to his supporters and the crowd. Then John and his family approach the podium.

John looked out over the crowd as they clapped politely. He estimated that about one hundred people were there, including a handful of his students. John thanked everyone for being there and introduced a few important people, including his wife, children and grandchildren, and Hank Johnson, who would be his campaign manager. John also introduced Dr. William Randolph, John's twin brother, who would serve as his chief of staff. John gave the following speech:

My name is John Robert Randolph, and I am running for president of the United States.

Over the last four to five years, our great country has been struggling. It first started with the bursting of the housing bubble, followed by the financial meltdown, then by bailouts and stimulus packages and unrestrained spending. It also included the passing of one of the most heinous pieces of legislation in history, the health care reform act. Since 2006, the debt has risen from $8.5 trillion to more than $14.5 trillion in less than five years. Just over the last three years, it has risen by over $4.5 trillion. What have we to show for that spending? Unemployment over 9 percent, a weak US dollar, $4 per gallon gas prices, and an economy that cannot get any traction.

I am here to say that our president's economic policies have failed America. It is time for leadership. It is time for career politicians to get out of the way and let someone else run this country. It is time for a successful businessman to run this country. It is time to tell the American people the truth—that our current entitlement structure is not sustainable; that our spending is too high; that in some specific cases our taxes are too low and in other cases they are too high. It is time to get the politics out of our government and put the focus back on the American people. It is time for a true change in Washington.

163

Over the last several years, I have developed a nine-point plan to fix America. It will not be easy and will take time. I am not arrogant enough to say that I have all the answers, but I have a starting blueprint to get the discussion moving. The nine points are broken down as the critical three and the big six.

Before we can fix the problems of our country, we have to fix some of the structural problems that have prevented us from making favorable progress on our problems. Congress must pass comprehensive lobbyist reform that will stop the buying of influence in Washington. This will be a hard thing to accomplish because there is so much money sloshing around in PACs and reelection bank accounts. If we stop lobbyists' money, politicians will focus on those who put them in office. Secondly, we must have campaign finance reform. In the 2008 presidential election, candidate Barack Obama spent over $700 million for a job that pays $450,000. How does this make sense? I am announcing my candidacy one year and seven months before the election. The election cycle is too long and too much money is wasted slinging mud back and forth among the candidates. This needs to be fixed. Thirdly, we need a constitutional amendment placing term limits on Congress. It is utterly ridiculous for a person to go to Congress and spend thirty, forty, or even fifty years in office. The founding fathers did not envision a place where people make careers. It is time for Congress to have term limits, thus enabling fresh ideas to continually circulate the body.

Once we put these items in place, we will be more successful in achieving the big six. The first item is entitlement reform. Over the last twenty years, entitlement programs have expanded much faster than the overall economy. They now comprise over half of the country's tax revenues, and they are expected to grow to over two-thirds in five to eight years. The fact of the matter is entitlements have become a way of life, as opposed to what they were created to be—a means to give a temporary helping hand. I want to make it abundantly clear to everyone who is listening. I am not proposing nor will I ever propose the removal of Social Security, Medicare, or Medicaid from current recipients or those in need. I am saying that it took several generations to get us where we are today, and it will take at least one generation for us to break the cycle.

The second item is true health-care reform. The first step in this is to repeal ObamaCare on the first day in office. Over 85 percent of Americans have health-care insurance. Ten percent have the option of having insurance but for whatever reason do not purchase the insurance. The remaining 5 percent do not have access to health insurance. President Obama is willing to destroy the best medical system in the world so that 5 percent can have coverage. Now I agree that health-care costs have risen much more rapidly than the economy and that substantial changes are needed. I believe that the first way to deal with runaway costs needs to be reforms in our tort laws. Doctors spend over 20 percent of their practice costs on insurance to protect themselves from vultures. Tort reform would save costs immediately throughout the entire health-care system. We need to have portability of health insurance between states. This will give consumers more choices and when more competition is present, better prices. We need to get rid of the ineffective regulations that plague our health-care system, and allow doctors to treat patients instead of filling out ridiculous forms. And we need to change the way we look at insurance. I have automobile insurance for my car, but when I need gas or an oil change, I pay for that myself. Our medical insurance needs to work the same way. When I get a cold, I need to pay for doctor visits myself. These are but a few ideas that I have on reforming health care without throwing the baby out with the bathwater.

The third step is to introduce new rules for spending and taxes. Read my lips: earmarks must go. Every appropriation needs to stand on its own. If someone believes the only way a certain appropriation can get passed is by pasting it on another bill, then that expenditure should not be made. We need to have a law stating that for any new spending increases, the originator must have a substantiated way to pay for it. There should be a law that for any new tax increase, the originator must provide options for spending cuts equal to three times the amount of the tax increase. Conversely before any tax decrease, the originator must substantiate equal spending cuts to offset the *lost tax revenues. Finally, we must have a balanced budget amendment immediately because we are unable to control our nation's credit card.*

The fourth step calls for the disbanding of the Department of Education and to move the function to the individual states. The Department of Education has been a failure. We continue to throw more money at education year after year and the results? Horrid! Back in the 1950s, American students tested extremely well as compared with students around the world. Today, America spends more than any other country per child on education yet test scores have America in the lower twenty-fifth percentile of the world. How did this happen? By taking the focus off the child and putting it on a federal bureaucracy. This must be one of our most pressing areas of focus.

The fifth step is to make public unions illegal. In private companies, the union personnel negotiate with either the owners, or proxies to the owners. In public union negotiations, both parties are represented by the union. That is why, on average, employees of public unions are paid twice as much as their counterparts on the private side. It is unfair for taxpayers to be taken advantage of like this, and it must be changed.

Finally, the sixth step is a complete change in the tax code. I am proposing a flat tax without any deductions and with a lower tax rate. This will allow finding tax cheats much easier and allow everyone to pay their fair share. No longer will lobbyists have a say in who wins the tax lottery and who does not.

This is how I would go about fixing America. As I said, it will not be easy, and there will be shared pain on everyone's part. My campaign will begin publishing my nine point plan in a brochure today. I look forward to comments from my challengers, including Democrats. I am sure I will be painted as a fanatic. But as long as you call me a truthful fanatic, I will accept the name.

I have been extremely fortunate in my life. I was born with a twin brother into a middle class family in South Hill, Virginia, and was educated at the College of William and Mary, where we are standing right now. I went to work at Smith Goldman and achieved success by working and studying as hard as I could. I married an incredible woman and my best friend, Jenny, with whom I share two lovely children. Nothing was given to me other than opportunities. Last October, I retired from Smith Goldman, and moved back to my beloved Virginia, where I started to teach a class on capitalism.

Over the last two and a half years, as I watched the American dream vanish for so many Americans, I started to imagine what I could do to fix America. I figured that this country, which has been so generous to me, needs for me to give back. I was never interested in politics as a profession, but I am *extremely interested in fixing America. I want to use the knowledge and wisdom that I learned as the CEO of Smith Goldman to make America successful. We can do this together. It will be tough and painful at times. But the America that I know is made up of exceptionally strong-willed, determined people who refuse to lose or back down because a problem has become too difficult. It is time to unleash American talent and tenacity on these problems and fix America. I look forward to seeing you as I campaign, and I sincerely hope that I can earn your support. God bless you, and God bless America.*

Chapter 45

John put his suitcase in the car then sat in the passenger seat. Jenny had already started the car, and soon they were heading down the driveway. Both were unusually quiet as they drove to the Richmond Airport, about thirty minutes from Williamsburg. John was getting ready to board an airplane and start an exciting but scary journey to introduce himself and his plan to the American people. Jenny was wondering if John was going to be liked and how the public would receive his message.

As they got closer to Richmond, they started talking about the upcoming day's events. John was meeting with some Republican leaders in Des Moines, Iowa, and Hank had already set up a dinner time speech with a VFW chapter. John was planning on introducing himself at several meet-and-greets later in the day. Hank had left Virginia yesterday to get things started in Iowa. William was busy setting up a campaign office in Williamsburg. There were a lot of things going on at once, and many more things to do. This was the launch the Randolph campaign; John hoped he'd soon be a household name.

As the car pulled in front of the airport, John reached over to kiss Jenny and thank her for her unending support. She told him how proud she was and encouraged him to work very hard in spreading his message. John told her that he would miss her. They exchanged smiles, and Jenny watched him walk into the airport. She said a little prayer before driving back to Williamsburg.

As the airplane moved into takeoff position, the pilot announced their ready status. John knew he was ready for takeoff too. He was ready to win this election for America.

John Robert Randolph for President
How to Fix America
A Nine Point Plan

We have a lot of problems now in America. We have runaway spending by the president and Congress. We have an extremely poor economy, a Congress more intent on preservation than looking out for America, and a president more interested in vacationing and talking a good game than truly leading. The problems in America did not just happen, and they are not easy to fix. There are underlying situations that must be fixed before tackling the problems.

In order to fix America, I have developed a nine point plan. The first three items must be done first in order to finish the list. I call them:

The Critical Three

1. Comprehensive Lobbyist Reform

Discussion
For every position that a member of Congress takes, you will find a lobbyist willing to support him or her financially for that position. Lobbyists come in every shape and size. Traditionally on the left are teachers' organizations, almost all unions, most lawyer associations, ACORN, and almost all environmental organizations. Business organizations, police unions, military organizations, and the Christian organizations typically support the conservatives. In the middle (in other words,

will support whoever supports them), are financial institutions, energy companies, and food companies. These groups spend whatever "soft" money is needed to get their organizations what they want. Buying influence is not a new concept at all, but it is terribly dangerous when you combine it with unlimited terms by members of Congress and extremely relaxed campaign finance rules.

Solution
In order to fix this problem, all lobbyists must register as such. Second, absolutely no money can be accepted by politicians—period. No contributions to their reelection campaigns, no contributions to their political action committees, no contributions to their foundations, no lobbyist paid lunches or boondoggles to exotic locations. If you eliminate lobbyists' money, you will correct about 50 percent of the problems in our current system of government.

2. **Campaign Finance Reform**

Discussion
Campaign finance rules are a complete joke. At their inception, the rules were developed assuming that every politician was honest and practiced ethical behavior. Of course, this was a farce. Ever since then, campaign finance rules have been modified to correct deviant behavior by politicians. Since campaigns have been entities unto themselves, the campaign sessions have extended.

Barrack Obama started campaigning for president at the beginning of 2007.

Solution
The most powerful thing to do to fix campaign finance rules is to eliminate soft money completely. If politicians can only accept contributions of $2,000 per person, not only would the spending decrease but the length of the process would also decrease. Once each of the parties has decided on a candidate at the beginning of September, each candidate must agree to the federal spending limits. This will eliminate the super wealthy from having an unfair balance through the elimination of soft money. Finally, only campaigns can produce television advertisements.

3. **Term Limits for Members of Congress**

Discussion
The president of the United States is limited by the Twenty-second Amendment to the Constitution to two terms in office. However, Congressmen can serve for life. For example, Senator Robert Byrd, West Virginia, was in Congress for 50 years. Ted Kennedy was first elected Senator from Massachusetts in 1962 and served until his death in 2009. Ted Stevens served as Senator from Alaska from 1968 until his defeat in 2008. Is it healthy for the country to have legislators serving for twenty, thirty, or fifty years?

Solution
A Constitutional amendment needs to be drafted and put forth to the US voters. I propose that representatives can serve two consecutive terms. I further propose that senators can serve one term. After sitting out at least one term, the representative or senator could again run for office.

Once these three items are in place, the rest of the agenda will be much easier to discuss and pass.

4. Entitlement Programs

Discussion
This is the two-thousand-pound gorilla. Once the government has given entitlements, they cannot be eliminated. There are three parts to our entitlement programs that must be addressed. Since these programs began, every president has known that a time of reckoning was coming. But none wanted to deal with the political fallout of such a confrontation. In the next ten years, Social Security will be bankrupt, Medicare will be bankrupt, and it appears that ObamaCare will be bankrupt from day one. These programs are all Ponzi schemes; each requires one group to contribute to the government for the benefit of another group. They were poorly conceived at inception, and politicians since then have been negligent in not dealing with the upcoming problems.

Solutions

Social Security—For each person drawing Social Security today, there will be no change to your benefits. For people in their sixties, there will be no change to your future benefits. For people in the fifties, a graduated scale will be put into place so that your benefits will be lower than those in their sixties. For people in lower age groups, there will be a lowering scale. People who have not begun work yet will not have Social Security at all. It will take a full generation for the United States to get phase out Social Security. In addition, for people in their twenties through their fifties, there will be an income measure in the provision. If you make above a certain percentage or you have a net worth above a certain percentage, you will not receive benefits.

Medicare and Medicaid—For persons already on Medicare, there will be no changes to your program. For people between fifty and retirement age, there will be a graduated scale on what you will be entitled to. This will include an income or wealth provision. Medicaid will continue to help people who cannot afford health insurance. This will require a serious change to health insurance (see below).

ObamaCare—Since the program does not take effect until 2014, the entire bill must be eliminated and replaced with the aforementioned details and Health Insurance Reform Act discussed below.

5. Health Insurance Reform Act

Discussion
Health care and health insurance are currently some of the biggest topics of discussion in the country. The concepts of socialized medicine, death panels, and birth to death coverage have taken over the discussion in this country. I have never seen a piece of legislation create as much fervor as ObamaCare. It is obvious that the majority of the country did not want it. It is equally obvious that the Democrats were willing to risk everything (and give anything) to see it pass. I agree that health-care costs have risen too fast as compared to other costs. I also agree that as a percentage of gross domestic product, health care comprises 20 percent and is rising. I also know that the United States has the best medical infrastructure that the world has ever known. More than 85 percent of Americans have health-care coverage today. Of the 15 percent of Americans who do not have coverage today, 10 percent could have it if they wanted. That leaves 5 percent without coverage. Democrats are willing to destroy the best medical system in the world for 5 percent of the population. It simply makes no sense.

Solution
There are several things that must be done to fix healthcare in this country.

a.   Tort Reform—we must eliminate class action torts from the legal system in this country. We must limit the awards patients can receive following medical errors. We must stop lawyers and patients from using the court systems as a de facto lottery. If you lose your case, you must pay the defendant's legal costs plus a 15 percent adder.

b. Allow Insurance Transferability—We must eliminate the state rules on insurance transferability. Currently, if you want to purchase an insurance policy, you must purchase a policy that is applicable in your residing state. If another insurance company creates a policy that is cheaper but not applicable in your state, you cannot apply for it. By eliminating the current state rules, additional competition will be created, which will lower costs to the consumer.

c. Concept of Insurance—We must change our way of thinking about health insurance. Currently, a decent health insurance program will pay for everything that the doctor charges. The patient is responsible for copayments and deductible amounts. Car insurance only deals with big items such as collisions, weather damage, and so on. Car insurance does not cover oil changes, car washes, transmission overhauls, and so on. Health insurance should be similar; it should not pay for normal office visits, visits due to colds or flu, and so on.

d. Eliminate ineffective regulations that overburden doctors and hospitals.

e. Eliminate red tape at the Federal Drug Administration. Currently, the United States is the slowest country in releasing new drugs as compared to other members of the G20.

f. Allow drug companies to write-off drug research faster so patents on new drugs can be obtained more quickly, allowing generic drugs to be produced faster.

6. **Earmarks and Spending by Congress**

Discussion
Congress is responsible for spending in the United States, but certain new rules are needed to regulate Congressional ethics.

Solutions

a. No new spending without a means for paying for it. This must be verified by the Congressional Budget Office before the spending happens.

b. No new tax cuts without a means for paying for it. This also must be verified by the Congressional Budget Office before the tax cuts occur.

c. Develop a plan to balance the budget (a proposal can be found in Appendix A). New budgets must include the interest on the old debt. Increases in the debt ceiling require two-thirds approval from Congress and approval by the president.

d. After enactment of the one-time new revenues and spending cuts, any future new revenues must be accompanied by two times the amount of spending cuts.

e. Earmarks cannot be added to any bills going forward. All spending must be transparent and part of spending bills.

f. Congress cannot give themselves salary increases going forward. This responsibility should be given to the president.

g. All spending bills in the future must be segregated by state and district. No one with a vested interest in a spending provision can vote for the measure. For all bills that include sweeteners (future promises for future benefits), those must be documented within the first two pages of any new bills.

h. The Congressional Budget Office must prepare a biannual report showing the amount of money being spent in each district and state. The amount of tax revenue generated by that district must also be shown.

i. Congressional and presidential personnel must have the same entitlement programs as the rest of the American people. No future pensions for life, and so forth.

7. Disband the Department of Education

Discussion
The creation of the Department of Education was a farce at inception, and it has failed in its charter. Test scores of US children have decreased every year since the creation of the department.

Solutions
a. The reduction in headcount and infrastructure costs should be given to the states.
b. A non-compensated board of state educators should be elected to serve as an advisory committee to set goals and standards for the country for precollege education as a whole.

8. Disband Public Unions

Discussion
Public workers unions are illegal. The negotiation between a union member and the union for wages and benefits for the group is similar to a fox guarding the chicken coop. If public unions want to negotiate, it must be with the taxpayers of America since they are the owners of America.

Solution
Eliminate all public worker unions.

9. Modify and Simplify the Tax Code

Discussion
Currently, the US tax code is a series of rules with exceptions and exceptions to the exception. The code is complicated and hard to comply with. Billions and billions of dollars are spent to prepare tax returns and for enforcement activities.

Solutions
a.   A simplified tax structure needs to be put in place. The tax structure needs to be a combination a tax on income and a tax on consumption. The tax on income is similar to what's in place today. The tax rate should continue to be progressive but at lower rates. The tax on consumption is a national sales tax or value-added tax.
b.   Tax cheats should be punished more financially than with jail time. Asset possessions and garnishments should be the standard punishments. Once a week, the IRS should post on the Internet and publish in newspapers a listing of all tax cheats.
c.   Tax-rate changes must be approved by Congress and the president.

These nine points would focus Congress on their constituents as opposed to their reelections and their own self-interests. It would also "right the ship" on the country's financial situation. The current spending patterns and policy positions are simply the wrong direction for our country.

Appendix A
Proposal to Eliminate the Deficit

	In Billions	Comments
New Revenues:		
Reduce Corp Rate to 20%	$ (95.0)	Reducing the corporate tax rate from 35% to 20%
Addl Revenues GDP	150.0	will increase the amount of revenues by $55 billion.
Revenues from Countries		
Relying on our Military	150.0	Sharing the cost for the world's greatest military
4% VAT Tax	600.0	4% valued added tax on every aspect of economy
Flat Tax Structure	175.0	Eliminating deductions, lower tax rates
Total New Revenues	$ 980.0	
Spending Cuts:		
Discretionary:		
Defense	$ 305.0	Exit strategies for all conflicts
Education	130.0	Eliminate and move to the states.
Transportation (A)	21.6	
Protection (A)	19.5	
General Govt (A)	13.4	
Other Spending (A)	87.3	
Mandatory:		
Pensions	100.0	Increase the age or means testing.
Healthcare	100.0	Increase the age or means testing.
Welfare	250.0	Unemployment back to 33 weeks/eliminate fraud
Total Spending Cuts	$ 1,026.8	
Total New Revenues		
and Spending Cuts	$ 2,006.8	
Reduction in Debt	$ 361.5	
Years to Eliminate Debt	33.2	

A - Move back to spending levels in 2007.

	In Billions	Comments
Current Debt Level	14,500	
Sale of 250 million acres		US Government owns 780 million acres. Proposal
at $10k/acre	(2,500)	to sell land to reduce debt.
Revised Debt Level	12,000	

www.ingramcontent.com/pod-product-compliance
Lightning Source LLC
Chambersburg PA
CBHW061203170626
46809CB00003B/1225